To those who know that time is just a story

PROLOGUE

Names are powerful things few people know how to handle. When you name something, or someone, that thing or that person becomes the name itself. And then it can't be anything but the meaning it's bound to.

Stories begin with names and end with names. Without them, the fabric of a tale would lose its structure. No beginning, no middle, no end.

There aren't many things more powerful than a man who knows the inner truth of his own name. Except, perhaps, a man who possesses many names.

A man with many names is a harbinger of change because he can be many things at once—or nothing at all.

～

THE MORNING BROUGHT a stark wind that wormed between the buildings of the city like a never-ending snake. The cloudy sky spoke of rain to come, and the streets still wet spoke of rain that was already embedded in the past.

Everyone in the city was stirring, moving, preparing for the beginning of a new day. Everyone but him.

For him, a day was never young and would never grew old. It was not a ring added to the chain of history. It was a drop of water in a river.

He was a tall figure clad in black, wearing a beanie and a pair of sunglasses. He wore something else besides clothes. He wore many names, and he despised all of them.

Those names were stories someone else had attached to him. He was not fond of those stories. And yet he could not get rid of them. Names have a way of sticking, no matter what one does to get rid of them.

The building he was looking at also had a name.

It was the tallest structure in the city, made out of shining glass and steel so polished it was able to reflect the clouds in the sky. The building was less than one year old, and it gleamed like all new things presented to the world with pride.

It was magnificent, it was imposing, and it was indubitably pompous.

They called it the Spear, a fitting name for a building whose design seemed to thrust the sky with arrogance.

The figure clad in black was fascinated. The Spear was exactly what he needed, a wheat field ready to be harvested. It sheltered many names, each one with a story attached to it.

Those stories were filled with needs he could satisfy. For a price, of course.

He just needed a key to enter that vault, gather names around him, listen to their stories, and use them to his advantage.

The process of finding this key would be long and hard. He would fail many times over, and he would have to start anew.

The tall figure glanced at his wristwatch. The hands of the clock were still, trapped in the amber of the moment. He smiled an odd smile as he looked back at the Spear.

Failure didn't matter to him. Every endeavor requires an investment of time, and he was willing to use all he had for the promise of success.

❧

THE MAIN ENTRANCE of the Spear had two security guards. One was tall and muscular. His name was Logan. The other one was even taller and, if possible, even more muscular. His name was Bob.

They looked equally bored with their job.

Nothing ever happened inside the Spear. Or in front of it. Or anywhere on the property, for that matter. The role of the two security guards was a ceremonial one. They were well-dressed scarecrows paid by the hour to nod professionally when people placed their badges on top of an iron pillar that flashed with a green light, granting them access inside the building.

It was a few minutes before nine o'clock in the morning. Nine was when the workday at the Spear began.

A short man with a balding head came running toward them. He stopped a few feet away from the entrance, bent over to catch his breath, hastily scanned his ID and made his way in.

"Rush hour's over," Logan declared, glancing at his cell phone.

"Uh-huh," Bob said.

"Looks like it's going to be another rainy day, eh?" Logan looked at the sky, rubbing the back of his head lazily.

"Guess so." Bob shrugged. "How's Betty?"

"Complaining about her yoga teacher," Logan said, scratching his carefully trimmed beard. "Again. She said the yoga mat stinks, the blocks stink, the bolsters stink. Even the damn mirrors stink, she said."

"She pregnant or something?" Bob asked, fighting a yawn.

Logan seemed to think about that for a while. "Nah," he finally said, waving the thought away.

Silence washed over them.

"I'm going to take a piss," Logan said, turning away.

"You got it."

Bob inhaled sharply and then yawned a long, satisfying yawn.

Something black caught the corner of his eye. He turned toward the inside of the building.

A tall man stood a few feet past the fancy glass entrance of the Spear. He was wearing a long black raincoat, a black beanie, and a pair of sunglasses.

His gloved hands held a bulky DSLR camera.

Bob blinked and looked around. He glanced at the entrance he had been guarding, then he looked back at the man with the camera and started walking toward him.

"Sir?" he said in a firm tone.

The tall man didn't seem to hear him. He raised his camera, pointed it at a man who was heading to one of the many elevators, and took a shot.

"Excuse me, sir," Bob said, this time more loudly. "Pictures are not allowed inside the building."

"Really?" the man didn't look at Bob. He shook his head while looking at the picture's preview. "Too much time left to this one," he mumbled dismissively. He scanned around and took the picture of another person a bit farther away. "And why is that so, young man?" he asked absentmindedly.

"Security reasons," was Bob's flat reply.

"Security reasons?" the man mused. Again he studied the picture's preview. This time he smiled a broad smile. He finally looked at Bob. "Whose security?" he asked, sounding puzzled. "My security? Yours? The system's security?" He spread his arms wide, as if pointing to the whole world. "You ought to be more specific if you want me to take seriously this *security* of yours."

"How did you get in?" Bob asked, pointing to the entrance.

"Through the front door," the tall man said.

"No, you didn't." Bob took another step forward. "How did you get in?"

"I told you," the man insisted. "I used that entrance."

"I didn't see you."

The man shrugged. "I surely hope you did not, otherwise you'd be far more interesting than you look."

"I—" Bob cut himself off. There was something odd about that man. He couldn't put a finger on it. He didn't look like somebody who worked at the Spear. "Sir, I need to ask you—"

"What is your name, young man?" the man interrupted.

"What was that?"

"Your name. What is it?"

Bob frowned at the unexpected question. The stranger seemed genuinely curious to know his name. He had put away his camera and was studying the security guard.

"Bob," the guard finally said. "Listen up. You—"

"Bob." The tall man nodded thoughtfully, as if a dark secret had finally been revealed. "The diminutive form of the name *Robert*. Also a diminutive of *Bobby*. Do you know the story of your name, Bob?"

"What?"

"It has ancient roots, buried deep inside European history. Your name started as a colorful pastime. Rhyming names was a popular practice in the Middle Ages. That is how William became Will, Bill, or Gill, and Robert became Rob, Hob, Nob, or Bob. The craftsmanship of names is a fascinating art. Also a dangerous one. Do you know why, Bob?"

"Sir, I'm asking you to—"

"I'll tell you why," the stranger continued with resilience, unconcerned with Bob's peremptory manners. "The meaning of a name plays a huge role in the life of a person. It shapes their story and can affect everything they do."

Bob opened his mouth, but nothing came out of it. It was a split-second hesitation, during which the stranger raised a hand to gain Bob's attention. "The people you meet," he continued, "the action you take, the woman you love. Everything in life is influenced by the power of a name. Your name is quite boring, though, and frankly, I didn't expect anything else from a person feeding so much of his time to this place."

Bob held out his hand. "I'm going to need that camera, sir."

"This?"

"Yes, sir. That one."

"Here. Take it." The man handed the camera to Bob.

Bob stepped forward to take it, but the stranger drew his hand back and met Bob's eye.

"But first," the man said, wearing a wide smile, "don't you want to know my name?"

Bob had had enough of that.

"Control?" he spoke into his radio. "I've got a seven-oh-one in the—"

He never finished the sentence.

Instead, he found himself rubbing his chin absentmindedly in front of the entrance door of the Spear.

He looked around, lost for a second. How did he get there?

"Rush hour's over," Logan declared, glancing at his cell phone.

Bob turned sharply to his right, where he found Logan staring at nothing.

A long, tense moment passed before Bob said awkwardly, "Yeah." He glanced at his phone. It was nine o'clock. "It is."

"Looks like it's going to be another rainy day, eh?" Logan looked at the sky, rubbing the back of his head lazily.

"Guess so," Bob said, like he was reading lines from a well-known script. He glanced behind him, where just a few seconds before he thought he'd seen somebody. "How's Betty?" he felt impelled to ask.

"Complaining about her yoga teacher," Logan said, scratching his carefully trimmed beard. "Again. She said the yoga mat stinks, the blocks stink, the bolsters stink. Even the damn mirrors stink, she said."

"She's pregnant, or—" Bob paused, glanced back again, and looked at his colleague with a confused expression.

"You okay?" Logan asked.

"Wait a sec," Bob said. "Didn't we have this conversation before?"

"Sure we did." Logan grinned. "We have it every day. Hey. What's up, buddy? Having a little déjà vu?"

Bob stared at Logan. "Yeah," he said after a moment, smiling sheepishly. He nodded, as if convincing himself of something. "I guess so."

"I'm going to take a piss," Logan said.

"You ... You got it."

Logan walked away, chuckling.

Bob was left looking around aimlessly, wondering about something that had never happened.

1

A GRAY MAN

Alfred White woke up to the sound of an alarm clock. He rose from his bed in a fluid motion, picked up his phone from the bedside table, and turned off the alarm. He then looked at the display with bleary eyes; it was seven thirty in the morning.

He yawned. His jaw cracked a few times, and he stretched with a moan, got off his bed, and headed to the bathroom.

From the partially opened window came the noise of cars moving, occasionally honking, and the soft, muffled rapping of dewdrops.

His home was on the second floor of five in a building located near the city center. Alfred could hear people talking in the street. He grasped fragments of their conversations. Sometimes at night, when the city was quiet, the cars were fewer, and the shops were all closed, a homeless person would shout something in the darkness, and Alfred could hear everything as if the man were right beside him. It wasn't easy to sleep with that constant noise in the background, but Alfred liked the place because the rent was cheap and the building was just a few blocks away from his new workplace.

His workplace was the reason he had moved into the city. He didn't know a single soul there and had no idea if he would like it, but being accepted to work at the Spear was reason enough to pack his things and start a new life.

Working at the Spear had proven stressful and time consuming. He had to pass a half-dozen interviews with a half-dozen different people just to have the privilege to finally get in front of his project coordinator, whom Alfred had to impress quite a bit before finally landing the job.

You don't get to work for the third-biggest company in the country without sweating blood, but now that Alfred had finally earned his cubicle on the twenty-fourth floor of the Spear, he felt things would only get better.

There was a big mirror in his bathroom where he used to check his reflection before heading out. But he had stopped looking at it several days ago.

He knew too well what he'd see: dark eyes besieged by shadows, hollow cheeks, skin that had slowly turned more white than pink, and deep lines on his forehead that made him look much older than he was. He knew his body was thin and getting thinner. He had lost almost ten pounds in the last couple of weeks.

Alfred didn't care much. He knew his physical decay was a temporary thing caused by the stress of moving to the big city and by the many demands of his new job.

Soon enough he would get used to the fast-paced rhythm of his new life. He was fine. Everything was going to be fine. He just needed to settle in, get comfortable, and learn to go with the flow.

It didn't occur to him that he'd had the same mental conversation the day before.

And the day before that.

He finished up in the bathroom and headed back in to get dressed.

He opened his wardrobe. Five white shirts flanked five steel-gray jackets and five pairs of steel-gray trousers. Alfred picked up one jacket, one pair of trousers, and one shirt and started dressing.

When the top button of his shirt had been buttoned, Alfred picked up a small gel container and combed his hair.

He picked up a black umbrella from a coat hook by the front door and left his home feeling more tired than when he had come back the night before.

~

IN THE MORNING SKY, countless iron clouds moved slowly toward a sun already stifled by grayness.

A stark wind blew from the north. It moved the branches of the leafless trees lined up along Main Street as Alfred walked down the wide boulevard. They were some of the leanest, barest trees he had ever seen, their trunks a dark brown that reminded him of mud.

Many other people were walking. They were all hurrying to their destinations, occasionally glancing around but mostly looking at their cell phones, their eyes intent on the devices' colorful images, messages, and notifications.

Alfred blended in very well with the rest of them. He checked his cell phone and perused the Web. Just another gray man, wearing a gray suit on a gray day.

Eventually he arrived at the intersection of Daw and Main. The local street newspaper vendor, a woman in her late forties with long, tangled hair, wearing a worn coat and a pair of heavy rain boots, was shouting.

"City council approves tax break!" the woman announced, waving a bunch of newspapers toward the passersby. A few stopped to buy one and moved on.

At the second intersection, Alfred turned left onto a narrower, less crowded street, at the end of which a food truck was selling something sweet that looked a lot like crispy crepes.

Alfred had never really gotten the name of the food right. The vendor, a short old lady from Thailand with a broad face and an easy smile, had told him the name the first time he bought one. To him it sounded a lot like *kanbuag* or *kannung*. Now, when Alfred ordered one, he just called it a *kanny*.

Alfred rather enjoyed kannies, and they had been his breakfast since he'd moved into his new apartment.

He waited in line, a very long line. The food vendor was getting more popular by the day.

Once in front of the Thai lady, she smiled at him as always.

"Sawatdee ka," she greeted him. "Usual today?"

"Yes." Alfred rubbed his hands eagerly. "One kanny, please."

The lady busied herself and, after a few seconds, handed him the crepe filled with white cream.

"Extra cream today," the lady said. She gestured hastily toward Alfred's stomach. "You thin. And pale, eh? Need more food. Eat more, okay?"

"You're right," Alfred said, smiling. "Thank you."

"How work goes, eh?" she asked while wiping her hands with a towel. "Busy, busy?"

"Always," Alfred said, repeating the conversation they had most mornings. "You too, I see." He glanced over his shoulders. "I think you've got the whole city in line for your kannies."

"Cheap food," she said, nodding approvingly. "Good food. I make them happy. You know, customers talk to friends. They come to me for more. I take care of them. They take care of my bills."

"And the world is a happier place." Alfred handed her a ten-dollar bill.

"Too much," the woman said, waving the money away with a polite but altogether weak effort.

"I insist," Alfred said, holding the money for her to take.

"Young man is good man," the lady said, broadening her already-wide smile while pocketing the money. "Every day he's so generous. He makes me rich."

"You're welcome," Alfred said. "You have a great day."

While walking back to Main Street, Alfred thought that the Thai lady might have a point. He had always been a good tipper. How much money had he spent on kannies up to this point? He never really thought about that. Daily expenses like those could add up pretty quickly.

Alfred decided he would tally up all the money he spent on food from that day on. He took his cell phone out of his pocket to write the memo down, but once the display turned on, he forgot his resolution entirely and instead started browsing the Internet. He typed a web address and started shopping for a pair of shiny, black shoes he really needed for his new job. His project coordinator had pointed out that his shoes were the wrong black. Alfred didn't think there was anything wrong with them, but of course he didn't want to upset his boss. So the past couple of days he had spent most of his free time trying to find the right pair at a fair price. Unfortunately, all the shoes his project coordinator had suggested were very expensive, and Alfred was reluctant to buy them. But he knew he could delay no longer. He could not risk becoming the black sheep of the office just a few weeks after getting the job. He had learned that blending in as fast as possible was the only way to survive in his workplace, and so he kept looking at the cell phone's screen, his last shred of reluctance crumbling under the heavy pressures of his new life.

His phone notified him that his purchase had been completed as he arrived at the end of Main Street and the center of downtown, where the buildings were taller than anywhere else in the city.

Steel and glass and concrete made up that world of stores, sidewalks, and traffic lights. But there was something more, if one looked carefully enough, and Alfred was looking very carefully at that moment.

A block away from the end of Main Street there was a tall gate with a metal plate, a welcoming note engraved upon it: "Welcome to Aion Park: Green Oasis at the Heart of the City."

Beyond the gate, there was a sizeable park enclosed in a tall, wrought-iron fence.

Alfred walked toward that sign and past the gate, entering the green oasis. He was soon surrounded by trees, ponds, and chirping birds. The difference from the rest of the city was striking. It was almost like walking on another planet. A few people walked their dogs. Mothers with strollers shushed crying babies, and children scurried around freely on skateboards and roller skates.

Alfred had discovered the park less than a week before while looking for a shortcut to his workplace. Because he didn't have a car and wasn't a fan of public transportation, he had been very happy to discover that cutting through the park saved him almost ten minutes of walking.

Alfred breathed in the fresh air, pulled his phone from his pocket, and went back to browsing.

"Excuse me, young man. Do you know what time it is?"

Alfred stopped and looked up. On his left, a man sat on a bench surrounded by lemon trees. He was looking at Alfred from behind a pair of dark sunglasses, his lips curved in an odd smile. The man wore a thick raincoat the color of coal, which covered him from neck to knee. A beanie of the same color covered his forehead and ears.

"I'm sorry." Alfred glanced around, looking confused. "Were you talking to me?"

"Indeed, I was," the stranger said, nodding. "I was inquiring about the time, if you would be so kind." He pointed at Alfred's cell phone.

"Sure," Alfred said. "Sorry, I was just ... I was distracted." Alfred noticed that the man was wearing a wristwatch. "Oh," he said, indicating the wristwatch. "Did it die on you?"

"This?" the man brushed his wristwatch with a gloved hand and shook his head slightly. "This is working just fine, but it doesn't keep the time. Not anymore."

Silence followed. Alfred decided the man had made some kind of joke he didn't understand, so he smiled briefly, cleared his throat, and glanced at his phone. "Well," he said, "it's a quarter to nine."

"Good," the man said, looking pleased. "And would you happen to also know today's weather?"

Alfred frowned. "Well ... I ..." he trailed off while the man looked at him expectantly. Alfred examined the sky, still crowded with clouds. "I think it's pretty obvious that it's going to rain."

"Is that a personal feeling or what your clever device suggests to you?"

Alfred glanced at his cell phone. "Both, I guess."

"So you're *guessing* what today's weather might be. That doesn't really answer my question. I'm still not sure if it's going to rain today."

Alfred blinked. "I don't think there is a definitive answer to that question, sir. That's why it's called a weather *forecast*."

"Forecast," the man repeated as if tasting an extremely bitter fruit. "Wouldn't it be nice to know it for a fact?"

Alfred stood there, speechless. Before he could say anything else, the man pointed at Alfred's half-finished breakfast.

"Are you enjoying your *khanom buang*?" he asked.

"What was that?" Alfred frowned, taken aback by the sudden change of subject.

The man in black gestured toward his crepe. "That looks like one of the sweet delicacies sold by the lovely lady on Keeper Street. Am I right?"

"Oh, *this*?" Alfred looked at his breakfast. "Yeah, you're right. It's quite good, actually."

"It must be," the man said, lifting his arms up until he could lay them both over the back of the bench. "I saw you walking around here yesterday, and the day before yesterday. That was your breakfast every single time, wasn't it? You must be a young man with a knack for habits. You know, I like good habits too." He looked at a couple of people walking past. "I sit here and look at the good people of this city. People like you. Routine people. People who are never late. Always there when they are expected. Heading to work, I imagine?"

"Yes, actually," Alfred said. "I was just—"

"Must be a fine job," the man said, cutting him off smoothly. "Must be, if you are so careful to be on time every day."

"Well, it pays my bills," Alfred said, shrugging. He glanced at his phone and inhaled sharply. "I'm sorry, it's getting late. I have to go."

"Of course you do," the man nodded, as if Alfred had stated a universal truth. "Late is bad, always. It was nice to meet you, mister ..."

"My name's Alfred. Alfred White."

"Alfred," the man mused. "A modern descendant of the Anglo-Saxon name *Ælfræd*, formed from the binding of the Germanic words *ælf*, meaning 'elf,' and *ræd*, meaning 'counsel.' A common name. A name for royalty, artists, and entertainers. A name for kings. Pleased to meet you, Alfred White." The man stretched out his gloved hand and added, "Pacific."

"I'm sorry?"

"My name," the man said. "I'm called Pacific."

Alfred pocketed his cell phone, and the two shook hands.

"Have an incredibly ordinary day, young man," Pacific said, grinning.

The handshake lasted longer than Alfred expected, and Pacific's grip proved way too strong for his liking.

Alfred walked faster to make up for the time he had lost. But he had to keep himself from looking over his shoulder.

Pacific? What kind of name was that? Not to mention his clothes. He looked like a mixture of Neo from *The Matrix* and an undertaker. Definitely on the weird side. A few minutes later, Alfred reached the end of the park, walked through another gate, and once again found himself inside the world of steel and glass.

Right in front of him, an imposing skyscraper, shinier than a diamond, dominated everything. This was his workplace: the newest building in the financial district, the very symbol of the corporate world that ran the city, and the latest pride of the City Council. It was one hundred and eleven floors tall and made with enough glass to encase a small planet. They called it the Spear.

A stream of people headed toward the building, like an army of ants seeking the shelter of their anthill.

Alfred passed the entrance door, which was flanked by two security guards, and put his badge on top of an iron pillar that flashed with a green light, granting him access.

The inside of the building made everything and everyone seem small and insignificant. Alfred took one of the many elevators available and pushed the button to the twenty-fourth floor. The elevator was packed with silent people looking forward, their expressions completely blank. No one spoke. They hardly seemed to breathe. Some got off as the elevator stopped, and more came in.

On the twenty-fourth floor, Alfred got out of the elevator, walked through a maze of white corridors packed with white collars, and finally got to his cubicle, the one farthest away from the boss's office. The cubicle was furnished with a simple white desk, a computer, a chair, and a small paper shredder.

On his left, Jack Smith was typing on a keyboard. Jack was double his age and triple his size. His eyes were constantly dull, his shoulders hunched, and ever since Alfred had first seen him, Jack was frequently snacking on some kind of cheap food. That morning he was munching on wasabi peas while sipping absentmindedly from a coffee mug.

Alfred had spoken with him only twice since starting at the Spear: the first time to introduce himself, the second time to ask him where the bathroom was. Both times Jack had looked annoyed that his mouth was forced to do something other than chew.

Alfred looked away from Jack and glanced at the cubicle on his right. That was the dominion of Mrs. Debby Johnson, with whom Alfred had spoken only once, when she had pointed out that his typing was far too noisy for her liking. Alfred had apologized, of course, and had proceeded to type as quietly as possible.

The other people in the office mostly ignored him or pointed out things he was doing wrong, like wearing the wrong kind of tie, jacket, or hairstyle.

From their comments and their attitude, Alfred had learned a very important lesson: if you wanted to survive inside the Spear, you kept your head down and did as you were told. According to his project coordinator, Mr. Solidali, very few hires lasted a month inside the Spear. If you made it to the second month, only then you were considered to be more than a body that occupied space.

Alfred spoke with Mr. Solidali most. Mr. Solidali was a middle-aged man of average height with brown eyes constantly in motion, as if they were looking for something out of place.

He was the right hand of the boss, whose office was at the center of the twenty-fourth floor. Crossing him meant crossing the universe itself.

Alfred was about to sit behind his desk when he heard footsteps approaching.

"White?" It was his project coordinator.

"Good morning, sir," Alfred said cheerfully, smiling to his superior. Then he ventured, "How are you doing?"

Mr. Solidali disregarded Alfred's question and instead glanced at his wristwatch. "You're only five minutes away from the breaking point. Are you an adrenaline chaser, White?"

Alfred swallowed hard. *The breaking point* was the office term for *late*. And late meant death for people like Alfred, who aspired not only to make it to the second month but also to start a career at the Spear. "No, sir," Alfred said hastily. "I don't do adrenaline, sir. I'm as far from an adrenaline chaser as ... as ..." Alfred opened and closed his mouth comically, trying to finish the sentence in some clever way but coming up with nothing better than, "As an old man just a sneeze away from death."

Alfred broke in a nervous laugh. He stopped almost immediately.

Mr. Solidali looked at Alfred as if he were trying to decide something. In the end, he simply put a stack of paper on Alfred's desk and said, "I'm going to need a detailed analysis of this report by noon. Make it two pages long. Heck, no." Again he glanced at his watch and mumbled something. "Make it one," he ordered. "I don't have time for much fluff today. Gimme just the hard data this time, will ya? Keep off your sagacious remarks. Nobody needs to know the remarkably clever backstory of the word *incentivize*."

"Yes, sir," Alfred nodded. "Got it."

Mr. Solidali inspected Alfred's shoes as if an invisible presence had pointed them out to him. He pursed his thin lips, looked at Alfred as if the ozone depletion had been a devilry of his own device, and walked away with long strides.

Alfred sat behind his desk and sighed.

"Quiet, please!" came the shrill voice of Mrs. Debby Johnson.

"Sorry," Alfred said.

A loud sniff, and then the typing resumed.

Alfred started sorting the stack of papers.

Less than one hour later, he had completely forgotten about the man called Pacific.

2

THE TRICKSTER

Alfred White woke up to the sound of an alarm clock. He rose from his bed in a fluid motion, picked up his phone from the bedside table, and turned off the alarm. He then looked at the display with bleary eyes; it was seven thirty in the morning.

He followed his carefully planned routine as he did every morning. He showered, carefully avoided his reflection in the mirror, dressed, went out.

Once again, it was a cloudy day. The wind was even less forgiving than the day before, and the temperature had dropped drastically.

Alfred joined the river of people trickling onto Main Street and passed the usual newspaper vendor, who was yelling about increased housing costs. Alfred walked on Main for a while, turned left and got into Keeper Street. He waited in line and ordered his usual breakfast from the Thai lady.

The woman handed him the food with a smile that seemed copied and pasted from the day before. "Very nice shoes," she said, eyeing Alfred's brand-new black shoes approvingly. "Young man make more money, eh? He buys new things that make him even prettier." Her smile widened as her eyes narrowed.

"Well, thanks." Alfred blushed. He cleared his throat. "Yes, I bought them yesterday. Glad you like them." He paid in cash, tipping the woman even more nicely than he had the day before.

"See you tomorrow, yes?" the Thai lady said as she put the money in her pouch.

"You bet," he replied.

Alfred left Keeper and went back to Main Street. By the time he arrived in front of the park's gate downtown, his breakfast was long gone. A notification appeared on his phone while he was walking in the park; it was an incoming email from Mr. Solidali. The subject line began, "Read this now!"

Alfred stopped dead in his tracks, and his brain shut down as he focused on nothing except the message.

"Yet another good morning to you, Alfred White."

Alfred looked up from his phone. Right in front of him was the man he had met the day before.

"Hi." Alfred blinked several times then added, a bit lost, "I ... ahem ..." He trailed off for a few seconds. He didn't remember the man's name. Was it Perry? Potter, maybe? Alfred was really bad with names.

After a long silence, he smiled apologetically. "I'm sorry. I completely forgot your name."

"Pacific," the man filled in. "The name's Pacific. Like the ocean."

"Right, Pacific." Alfred gazed at his cell phone. "Good morning to you, sir."

"How are you faring today, young man?"

"Not too bad," Alfred said, nodding hurriedly. "Yeah, not too bad at all." He needed to get to work quickly. The breaking point was fast approaching, but somehow it seemed rude to leave the man like that. So he forced a smile and asked, "How about yourself?"

"Majestically well," Pacific replied. He tapped his wristwatch with his index finger. "Would you be so kind once more?"

"Wondering about the time again?" Alfred's polite smile was very tight. He was wondering if the man had nothing better to do than bother passersby with silly questions.

"Of course," Pacific said. "Is there anything more important than that?"

"Just out of curiosity, don't you have a cell phone?"

"A cell phone?" Pacific repeated, frowning. "Why should I have one?"

"Well, they're quite useful when it comes to talking to people." Alfred gestured toward his cell phone. "They are also quite handy for checking the time."

"See," Pacific said, settling back on the bench and casually smoothing his coat, "I meet the people I want to talk to in person. And regarding the time, why do I need a cell phone when I have you?"

That was it. Alfred decided the man was obviously more than a bit weird. Pacific kept staring at him like he was actually waiting for an answer.

"It's ten to nine," Alfred said dryly. He pocketed his phone and started walking away. "Have a good day."

"Ten to nine?" Pacific repeated, puzzled. "Are you sure?"

Alfred stopped and turned toward Pacific. "What was that?" he asked.

"I said, are you sure *that* is the right time?"

"Of course I'm sure." Alfred glanced back at his phone. "As I said, it's ten—" The words froze in his mouth. The display now showed seven thirty. He looked at Pacific then back to his phone. "I don't understand," he said, confused. He touched the screen a few times. The time didn't change.

"Is there a problem, young man?"

"I think so," Alfred said. He scratched his chin thoughtfully. "This damn thing is not working."

"Oh, the cell phone is fine," Pacific said, his voice deeper and graver than before. "The problem is the time, I fear."

But Alfred wasn't listening. He was too busy turning his phone off and on and praying that whatever had happened didn't happen again. He needed the damn thing to work, and he still had to reply to Mr. Solidali's message.

Alfred watched the home screen with anticipation.

"Ten to nine," Alfred said, sighing with relief.

"Good to know," Pacific nodded. "Time's a trickster if you don't know how to handle it."

Alfred put the phone back in his pocket. "My boss will kill me," he mumbled to himself. "I need to go now."

"Pray, young man," Pacific said, raising both hands. "Indulge me for one more minute and let me ask you a very important question."

"What question?"

"Would losing this job of yours really be the end of the world?"

Alfred narrowed his eyes suspiciously. "Beg your pardon?"

"It seems obvious to me you're fully invested in it," Pacific explained. "More than that, in fact. You're devoting your life to it. Why is it so important?"

"I work at the Spear," Alfred said flatly, as if that fact explained everything there was to explain.

"Ah. The Spear." Pacific looked impressed. "They say only the brightest minds work there."

"So I've heard," Alfred said, straightening up a little.

"I suppose one additional, foraging bee bringing pollen back to the hive is considered valuable to the overall system."

Alfred shook his head slightly. "What?"

"Nothing. Just thinking out loud. I don't want to keep you further. Of course you *need* to go. You don't want to be late. Off you go, then, Alfred White. Have another painfully average day."

Alfred walked away as fast as he could, trying not to look as though he were running.

While half walking, half running, he decided he didn't like that man. At all. He would take the longer way to work the next day and avoid the park altogether. He had better put that memo down in his agenda before he forgot.

A notification appeared on his phone. It was another message from Mr. Solidali. This one started, "Disregard previous message. Read this instead!" Once again Alfred's mind focused exclusively on the message. He kept walking and reading until he was in front of the iconic Spear and then on the twenty-fourth floor. There, a cubicle heavy with stacks of paper announced the start of a very long day of work.

3

DÉJÀ VU

Alfred White woke up to the sound of an alarm clock. He rose from his bed in a fluid motion, picked up his phone from the bedside table, and turned off the alarm. He then looked at the display with bleary eyes; it was seven thirty in the morning.

He felt tired. He had slept poorly the night before and lost many hours to his thoughts.

The previous day he had faced a problem at work, something he could not solve right away. Now he was afraid of Mr. Solidali's reaction. He would not be pleased. Alfred was certain of it.

This was a bad time for problems. His company was in the middle of the biggest project of the quarter, and they needed everything to run smoothly. Alfred knew he needed to solve the problem quickly. His survival on the twenty-fourth floor was at stake.

Alfred started preparing faster than usual. If he got to work sooner, he might be able to solve the problem before his project coordinator found out.

As always, Alfred followed his carefully planned morning routine, joined the stream of people walking on Main Street, passed the street newspaper vendor yelling about increasing rates of suicide, bought his breakfast, and finally headed toward the park.

By the time he passed the park's gate, his eyes were fixed on his phone's screen. He was studying a project's note that might help him solve his problem. He was focused on the task, his feet moving automatically, following the usual shortcut that would bring him faster to the Spear.

"A jolly good day to you, Alfred White."

Alfred's stomach sank to his feet as he looked in front of him, where an all-too-familiar face was smiling.

Right, Alfred thought. *This is the fucking icing on the cake.* He had completely forgotten about the annoying weirdo.

Alfred breathed in, thinking fast. He turned toward Pacific but kept walking. "Good morning, sir," he said, stretching the corner of his mouth in a smile while quickening his pace. "I'm terribly sorry. I'm in a rush and really can't talk with you today. I am very, *very* late for a meeting and I gotta go before I—"

"You're a liar."

Alfred stopped midstride and stared at the man in disbelief. "What did you just say?"

"I said, you're a *liar,*" Pacific repeated. There was no malice in his tone. He looked like somebody who had just made a comment on the weather.

"No, I'm not!" Alfred puffed his chest and glared at Pacific. "I'm just in a rush. That's all!"

Pacific frowned. "Why do you look so offended, young man?"

"*Why*? You just called me a liar!"

"Again, why so upset?"

"You called me a liar, and you're asking why I'm upset?"

"You're acting like I said something mean to you, but I didn't." Pacific looked at Alfred with a knowing eye. "Lying is a virtue if it's cultivated well. Your problem is that are a very *poor* liar, Alfred White. There you go. *Now* I'm being mean to you. See the difference?"

Alfred did not. He stared at the man who called himself Pacific and thought of something harsh to say back to him. However, he couldn't come up with something good enough, and that made him even more upset. He had never been good with quick remarks.

Alfred stood there, looking vaguely comic with his raised eyebrows and half-opened mouth.

"You said you *gotta* go," Pacific remarked, pointing in the direction Alfred was headed. "And you also said you're in a *rush*, as if time itself owns you. In fact, it's quite the opposite, but a poor rider will let a horse carry him if he has no idea how to use the reins."

Alfred had no clue what Pacific was talking about. Then again, the man was a few inches away from insanity. He was probably just a loony sitting on the same spot every day, hoping to snatch conversation from strangers.

Alfred considered his options. He had better things to do than waste time with this man. He needed to get moving.

And yet there was something that kept him standing there, something Alfred could not quite put a finger on. Was it because he wanted to get even with him? Was is it because of something Pacific had said? Or was it the way he had said it?

Pacific spoke again. "And of course you don't want to be late," he said. "Your reptilian brain forbids that. Doesn't it?"

Alfred glowered at him. "My *what*?"

"Your amygdala," Pacific explained. He touched the frontal portion of his temporal lobe. "It's the oldest part of your brain, responsible for primitive survival instincts like fear. Right now your amygdala is telling you to be in a rush. If you're not in a rush, you'll be late. If you're late, your boss will fire you. If he fires you, you won't have a job, which means you'll have no money to buy food, clothes, or shelter, and you will starve and die."

Alfred's heartbeat quickened.

Pacific's words resonated inside him like the tolling of a bell in the middle of a cave. They stormed like an invading army, crushing the walls of his soul and conquering his spirit.

Suddenly Alfred's rage collapsed into a fear with no name. It seized Alfred from the inside out and paralyzed him.

Pacific was right. That realization frightened Alfred so deeply and so quickly that his body started shaking. Every single word the man had said felt right.

But, just as urgently, his mind warned him he couldn't afford to listen to this man. He needed to get away from him. He needed to get back to work.

Alfred swallowed. He clenched his fists and looked at Pacific with contempt. Pride overtook him once again. "You don't know me," he retorted with defiance as his words betrayed him. "You have no idea who I am. I'm a busy person, and you're wasting my time. Don't ever talk to me again! You hear me? Leave me alone." Alfred started walking away without waiting for a reply.

A red ball hit him hard on the chest.

"Ouch!" Alfred exclaimed, recoiling.

The ball bounced three times on the grass before rolling toward Pacific. The man picked it up slowly.

A small boy no older than eight came running toward them. "I'm sorry, sir!" he said. "Can I have it back? Please?"

"Of course you can, miniscule fellow," Pacific said. He patted the child's head and handed him the ball. "Off you go, now. Adults are talking here."

"Thanks, sir." The boy ran away as quickly as he had come, disappearing behind a nearby bush.

Alfred was massaging his chest vigorously. The pain was still there. "That hurt," he said, wincing. "That freaking hurt."

"Bad karma, maybe?" Pacific seemed to enjoy Alfred's predicament. "You have quite a temper, young man, and no love for wise advice given freely. I was trying to make a point there, and that was no way to interrupt me."

Alfred snorted. "I don't care what you think." He started walking away.

He didn't get far.

Once again, a red ball hit him hard on the chest. "Ouch!" Alfred exclaimed.

The ball bounced three times on the grass before rolling toward Pacific exactly as it had before. The man picked it up slowly.

The same small boy came running toward them. "I'm sorry, sir!" he said. "Can I have it back? Please?"

"Of course you can, miniscule fellow," Pacific repeated. He patted the child's head and handed him the ball. "Off you go, now. Adults are talking here."

Alfred's mouth was wide open as he watched the scene unfold. Every word Pacific had said, every movement he had made, was an exact copy of what had already happened.

Alfred was no longer massaging his chest. He was no longer breathing, for that matter. He was staring at the boy as he disappeared behind the very same bush he'd gone through the first time.

There was no way Alfred could explain what had occurred. It was the weirdest thing to ever happen to him, like watching a movie clip twice in a row. Except he was not in front of a screen.

Alfred looked at Pacific, who sat with his arms folded, looking at the bush where the boy had disappeared.

"Marvelous thing, déjà vu," Pacific said. "An acquaintance of mine once described it as a 'tic of the time.' I'm not sure that's the most appropriate way to define it. However, when déjà vu occurs, it's always fascinating. And it's even more fun to create. Did you enjoy it?"

Alfred breathed in slowly. He looked at Pacific, then at the bush, then at Pacific again. "You ... You did that?"

"Of course I did." Pacific gave him a conspiratorial look.

Alfred's eyes narrowed. "H-How?"

Alfred knew the question sounded crazy. He wished he could take it back, but at the same time, he really wanted to know more.

Of course it didn't happen, said the voice of reason inside him. *You can't rewind real life.*

And yet it had happened. He had seen it with his eyes.

Déjà vu. Alfred let the words sink in. He was familiar with the concept, of course; he'd had his fair share of déjà vu before, but never like this. This was something completely different.

Pacific looked at Alfred behind his sunglasses. "*How*, you ask?" He paused, and patted the empty place on the bench beside him. "Well, if you want an answer to that question, young man, you won't go to work today. No, you will stay here with me, and we will talk."

Alfred's face was washed blank with confusion. "What?" he asked.

"You heard me, Alfred White. Take a day off. Do it, and I'll answer your question right here, right now."

Alfred flinched. "I ... What?" He took a step back without even realizing it. "Are you serious?"

"As serious as a corpse at a funeral." Pacific seemed amused by Alfred's puzzled expression. "What do you say? One day of your work in return for one day of knowledge. It's a steal. Get it while you can."

A nervous smile flashed on Alfred's face. "I ... I don't think so." He glanced at his phone. "I need to go."

"Why? You are dying to know the answer. I can see it." Pacific's hand was still patting the bench's empty spot. "You can take a day off and learn exactly what happened, or you can keep walking, go about your life, and never see me again. Do you really want that question nibbling at you for the rest of your life?"

Alfred stood there, speechless. "Nothing happened," he said stubbornly, stressing both words while trying to convince himself they were true. "*Nothing*. It was just ... just ..." he trailed off, not knowing how to end the sentence.

"Just déjà vu," Pacific filled in. "One. Short. Little. Déjà vu."

Alfred licked his dry lips, thinking of what to say, unsure of what to do.

The two men stared at each other while a daunting silence stretched, and time with it.

Pacific made a vague gesture. "No big deal, déjà vu. Just a nuisance." He raised an index finger. "But it can become much more than an inconvenience if you let it. You know why? It's because you can lose yourself in nothingness more easily that you can imagine. It happens fast. When your whole life starts to look like the same old movie, the daily routine and habits make everything look stale. The repetition, the copy-and-paste of one day onto the next, are like repeated cases of déjà vu carrying you closer and closer to the grave. Let me ask you this question: is your life starting to look like déjà vu, Alfred White?"

Alfred's heart bounded heavily against his chest. He knew,

inwardly, that Pacific was right. But admitting it would have been too much to bear. It would have meant denying his whole life up to that point. He couldn't afford that. And so he turned without replying and walked away from Pacific. Before he knew it, he was running.

When Alfred was well outside the park, he took his phone out of his pocket with a new resolution. He would never see that man again. Never.

This time he wrote the memo down, so that he would make sure to remember. He needed to stay away from that man, away from his madness.

When Alfred approached the gigantic building made of glass and steel, his heartbeat steadied. The Spear was something he could understand, something familiar, and it made him feel better.

It made him feel safe.

And he wanted no more than that now. He wanted to follow orders, to blend in, to be forgotten.

Alfred walked with long strides toward his safe harbor, past the stream of people, past the entrance of the Spear, and up to the twenty-fourth floor. He sought the security of the place where he spent most of his waking time, surrounded by like-minded people busy with tasks and moving with purpose.

Alfred finally entered his safe cubicle, his world inside the world, where a tall stack of papers was graciously waiting for him.

"Are you okay, White?"

Alfred whirled on the spot. It was Mrs. Debby Johnson.

"Yeah," Alfred said hastily. "I'm great. Thanks. Why?"

"You look ... paler than usual," Mrs. Johnson said, looking at him carefully. "And you're wheezing."

"I'm good," Alfred lied. "Bursting with health. Never been better. I swear. If you'd excuse me, I have work to do."

Alfred gladly embraced his work that morning and shielded himself from the unexplainable things that had happened in the park.

He successfully solved the problem he had faced the day before and looked for more things to do in order to keep his mind off Pacific.

Jack Smith had been sick for the past couple of days. It had started as a harmless cold but had turned into a fever, judging by Jack's shiny eyes. His colleague hadn't called in sick, of course, even thought he could have used a day off. You didn't call in sick on the twenty-fourth floor. You called in dead.

Alfred also knew that Jack was behind on a couple of project evaluations. He had overheard Mr. Solidali talking to him the previous day. Helping Jack looked like a great way to keep his head busy.

"You want to do it?" Jack said, a puzzled look creasing his forehead.

"I'd love to," Alfred answered with a bright smile.

"Why?" Jack asked. He looked surprised enough that he had stopped munching on his chocolate chip cookie.

"I've got nothing else to do."

"Are you done with the Jonny Case Cascade file?"

"Yup."

"What about the cross-functional roundabout?"

"Done and done."

Jack looked at Alfred intently. "Well," he said in the end, shrugging, "yes, sure. Help yourself." He cleared his throat. "And ... thanks. I guess."

"No," Alfred said, while quickly taking the USB flash drive Jack was handing him, "Thank you, kind sir." That said, he disappeared inside his cubicle.

It didn't take long for Alfred to finish Jake's assignment. When he was done, he looked around, wondering what else to do.

He heard the soft, rhythmic typing of Mrs. Debby Johnson just a few feet away. An idea bloomed in his mind. He peered over the partition into her cubicle. "Mrs. Johnson," he said as quietly as possible. She startled very easily. "May I speak?"

Mrs. Johnson's head jerked to the side so suddenly, Alfred thought her neck would break. "Isn't your brain aware of your mouth?" she snapped at him. "Can't you see you're already talking?"

"I'm sorry, Mrs. Johnson. Didn't mean to startle you."

"What is it that you want?"

"I ... I was just wondering if I could help you with your workload," Alfred said. "I know you've taken on Mr. Jolly's assignments while he's at the Seattle conference, and I thought I could help you with that, somehow ..." Alfred trailed off hopefully.

Mrs. Johnson's eyebrows rose. "You want to help me," she said.

"Yes, ma'am."

"Well," she said, looking doubtful, "that is very ... *kind* of you, White, but I don't think you've been around long enough to handle—"

"Try me," Alfred interjected, surprising himself with his boldness.

Mrs. Johnson was silent for a moment. "You've been here for ... ?"

"Over four weeks now," Alfred filled in helpfully.

"Right. And you know how to deal with a class-five deliverable?"

"I think I've got the gist of it. Mr. Solidali gave me a class seven yesterday."

"Did he, now?" Mrs. Johnson studied Alfred from behind her narrow spectacles, like she was seeing him for the first time. "Very well, then. I could surely use some help. I think Mr. Solidali believes there are three people working in this cubicle. Here." She handed him a file.

"Thanks, Mrs. Johnson," Alfred said, taking the file from her bony hands. "I'll give it to you in one."

"Day?" Mrs. Johnson frowned.

"Hour," Alfred answered.

Alfred pushed his chair forward and went back behind his desk, happy with his new task.

He wasn't aware his typing had gotten louder. Remarkably, no complaint came from Mrs. Johnson this time.

"Hey."

Alfred turned. It was Jack, leaning on his cubicle.

"Wanna grab something to eat at the bar?" he asked, sniffing. "I'm heading there now with a couple more folks."

"Thanks, but I'll pass," Alfred said cheerfully. "Maybe next time. I've got a deadline to meet."

"Sure thing." Jack cleared his mouth. "By the way, thanks again for the help. I owe you one."

"Don't mention it," Alfred said.

Less than forty minutes later, Alfred handed back the file to Mrs. Johnson, who looked at it diligently. When she closed it, she studied Alfred. "This will keep Solidali off my neck for a while," she said. "I guess I've misjudged you, young man. You do seem to have some hidden qualities, after all."

"I'm happy I could be helpful, Mrs. Johnson."

"Debby," the older lady corrected him, waving a hand like a queen granting one of her subjects permission to exist. "Just out of curiosity: why did you decide to do this kindness to me?"

"As I said, I just wanted to help. I had some time on my hands and—"

"Yes, sure," Mrs. Johnson interjected, smiling briefly. "But why, out of all the things you could have done, did you decide to help me?"

Alfred opened his mouth and closed it. He was genuinely speechless. "I'm not sure I understand—"

"Very well, then," the old lady said, her expression knowing. "Let's keep playing the low-profile game. I know a climber when I see one."

"A climber? Mrs. Johnson, I honestly—"

"You're young, and you're ambitious, and I'm not a fool," Mrs. Johnson said. "So let's just keep talking for a while, for the sake of it. Is that okay?"

"I-I guess so," Alfred stuttered, not really knowing what she meant.

Mrs. Johnson looked around as if to make sure nobody was listening. "As it seems you're going to stay with us for a while, let me give you a piece of advice. Be smart, and don't reach too far too quickly." The old lady pointed at a cubicle on the other side of the office. "We had a bright fellow a couple of months ago who believed he could skip the grunt work, go straight ahead, and charm Zeus himself." She glanced at the boss's office. "He was a fool who didn't know how things worked and never bothered learning. I've been here long enough to know this: if you want to open the shiny gates of Olympus, you don't bang at them. You bribe the gatekeeper. That's him." She glanced at Mr. Solidali's office. "Suck up to him, and then you might get your first taste of ambrosia. Have I made myself clear?"

"You have, Mrs. John— I mean, Debby. But I still don't—"

"Now," the woman continued inexorably, folding her hands and looking casually over her shoulder. "It happens that Mr. Solidali is facing a problem these days."

"A problem?" Alfred asked. "What kind of problem?"

"Let's just say he has a python strangling his neck, and has a deadline making things even more difficult for him. It might help you to know that the problem is the lack of a solid sales proposition for our King in the Moon client." She looked at the file Alfred had helped her fill. "Since it's pretty obvious to me that sales pitches are your strong suit, it might help you to pop into his office sometime today and offer to take a look at the very, *very* weak draft the marketing department has given him. I'm sure he could use some fresh ideas, and you seem to have plenty of them."

"Well." Alfred brushed away his hair from his eyes. "Thanks for the heads-up, Mrs. ... Debby."

"You're very welcome. You keep up the good work and avoid getting ahead of yourself, and I'm sure someone will notice. Lesson time is over. I'd better go back to work now."

Alfred went back to his cubicle.

He looked at the time. It was still three in the afternoon, and he had accomplished all his tasks. He started to think about Pacific, and about the impossible event that had happened that morning. But he shook his head and pushed the thought aside.

He glanced around with a new resolution and got a glimpse of Mr. Solidali before he entered into his office.

Alfred fidgeted for a few seconds. He glanced at Mrs. Johnson, rose, and walked to his project coordinator's office. He knocked twice on the door, was admitted, and asked his superior for more work. And Mr. Solidali, a man who had engraved on the door of his office the words "In work we trust," gladly obliged.

4

GOLD DIGGER

A lfred White woke at seven thirty as he did every morning. This time, there was a sheet of paper placed under the cell phone, with a message written in capital letters: AVOID THE MADMAN! DON'T GO TO THE PARK!

And Alfred didn't. He prepared for his day, went out, and did not take his usual breakfast, giving him extra time to walk the longer way to work.

He arrived at the Spear with a feeling of relief. Nothing out of the ordinary had happened that day. He would follow the same plan tomorrow, avoid the park altogether, and never see Pacific again.

One day followed the next faster than usual that week. Much faster.

Meanwhile, Alfred did everything he could to forget about Pacific and put much effort in reimagining the events that had happened the day of the déjà vu. He repeated to himself that what he *thought* he saw had been caused by stress or his imagination. One or the other. Or maybe both. Whatever. It just never happened the way he'd thought it had.

Alfred focused on his job more than ever. It became almost an obsession to him. Every morning, before going to work, he spent five minutes in front of the mirror repeating the same sentence over and over: "Work harder, forget what you saw, and stay away from that place." And he committed to long hours in the office, staying even after the last person had left. He buried himself under paperwork and became the most proactive person on the twenty-fourth floor, always looking for things to do, problems to solve, tasks to accomplish.

As time passed, his productivity and his confidence in his new job increased. Alfred was now able to deal with multiple projects at once, usually twice as fast as anybody else.

Mr. Solidali learned to trust Alfred the way he did the most senior staff. He was clearly pleased with the young man's skyrocketing performance, and told him so a couple of times.

Alfred's project coordinator was not the only one who looked at him differently. Alfred had proved what he was worth, and slowly but surely, new possibilities opened up for him.

People decided Alfred White was, after all, an okay guy who just wanted to be helpful and that was just trying to fit in.

As Alfred familiarized himself with his coworkers, some people even started to talk with him about their private life. It was amazing how, if they were stressed and tired enough, a person could open up and say all the private things that made their days miserable. Alfred learned, for example, that Dora from payrolls had a huge debt choking her up; that Mr. Brown from HR would have killed to get his daughter into the Golden Lock Private Academy for Art and Music but lacked the necessary connections to make it happen; and that Mrs. Shiva from merchandise had lost a fortune in the stock market due to impulsive investing and was now looking into real estate to compensate for her loss.

Every single person on the twenty-fourth floor had a story, and the more time Alfred spent with them, the more he understood that they put themselves into difficult situations they had no idea how to solve. And they loved to complain about them.

After several weeks of keeping himself busy, Alfred started to get the boss's attention. Yes, indeed, his boss was very pleased with his performance, Mr. Solidali said during one meeting. And the next day, to Alfred's surprise, the boss himself summoned him into his office.

"You're a good lad with fire in your belly," his boss said as soon as Alfred closed the door behind him. He was in his early sixties, very slim, almost bony, his face full of angles and his chin as sharp as a pyramid turned upside down. "Now, I understand Mr. Spencer hired you and put you in the prep and research department." He took a bite of a ham and cheese sandwich and resumed talking with his mouth full. "Is that right, Arnold?"

Alfred bit his lips, not knowing if it was wise to point out his real name. He decided to simply ignore the mistake and to reply with a polite, "Yes, sir."

"The man is an idiot." His boss spit into the trash bin then drank eagerly from a can of Coke. "He got a damn gold nugget as big as his fist and mistook it for brass. Unacceptable. I'll pop up to his office tomorrow and make sure he knows how displeased I am. He'll be on his toes for a month or two." He laughed a raucous laugh then took another bite of his sandwich and washed it down with more Coke.

Alfred said nothing. He just kept standing, hoping to look confident but knowing he looked, at best, just plain awkward.

"You're a thing of value, young man," his boss said, nodding approvingly. He put a finger inside his mouth and dug out a piece of ham that was stuck between his teeth. "I've asked around. People like you a lot, Arnold. Apparently, you have a knack for problem solving, and you are not shy when it comes to taking responsibilities. Isn't it right?"

Alfred cleared his throat. "I'm still learning, sir. I'm just trying to get my feet wet."

"Also modest," his boss said. "I'll have to add that to the list. Now, I've checked your profile and your opt-in score. Best damn percentile I've seen in a while. Not to mention that no one in your age group has received a score so high in the history of the marketing department. What are you doing with us, Arnold?"

Alfred was taken aback by that question. "I ... I don't understand, sir," he admitted, shifting weight from one foot to the other. "What do you mean?"

"Our company," his boss said. "What brought you to our firm? I mean, look at this." He indicated a number of sheets scattered on his desk. They all began with the title *Candidate #139—Inclinations and Expectations Evaluation.* "I see a number of different things you could have been in your life." His boss took a sheet from the pile and started reading it. "The opt-in test tells me volumes about your skill set. You could have been a terrific engineer, a cloud architect, a security trader. Anything better than this!" His boss spread his arms wide as if indicating the whole floor.

Alfred glanced around awkwardly. He felt like he was missing an important piece of information. "Sir," he said, "I'm not sure I'm following."

His boss frowned. "You're crammed all day inside a cubicle, filling out forms, for God's sake," he said, then paused, clearly expecting a reaction.

"Yes, sir," Alfred admitted. "That is correct."

His boss's eyes narrowed. "A trained monkey could do that."

Alfred imagined a monkey sorting papers and filling out forms. He started wondering if he was supposed to laugh to a joke he didn't understand. He studied his boss. His boss was not laughing.

"Sit down."

Alfred sat.

"I can't quite figure you out, son." His boss took another sip from his Coke. "Do you even know why you are here?"

"Not really, sir."

"You took on the assignments of half the damn floor, stuff you'd never been trained to do, and completed them in a few weeks."

Silence followed that statement.

Alfred swallowed hard. His boss's face was unreadable. "Is that ... good, sir?" he asked. His palms started sweating.

"Good?" his boss leaned forward. "You saved me almost one month of effort, Arnold, and proved that you could do the job of several people paid twice as much as you are. I call it remarkable—that is what I call it."

Alfred's tension loosened a bit. "I am ... glad to hear that, sir."

His boss grunted his approval. "We are the third biggest company in the country because of the hard work of people like you, who go above and beyond without being asked. You are a kingpin, son. Proactive people like yourself power up our brand and give us new lifeblood. I wish I had ten more guys with half your shine. So tell me." His boss leaned back on his chair and stared at him. "Where is all this drive coming from?"

Alfred moistened his lips. He was avoiding his boss's stare entirely, now. Instead, he was looking at the tips of his shoes.

"Well?"

For a split second Alfred considered telling his boss about Pacific to explain why he worked like a madman to simply avoid thinking. That was the truth, but somehow, the truth seemed out of place there, inside the office of the most powerful man on the floor.

So Alfred decided to provide his boss with the second-best answer he could come up with. The standard answer.

"I'm working hard to contribute to the well-being of the company," he said simply. "I hope, in the future, that my work will be rewarded."

His boss studied him then trashed what was left of his sandwich and the pile of papers on his desk. "Very good." His boss nodded, clearly satisfied with Alfred's answer. "That is what I thought. Now, let me tell you a story." The old man drained his pop in a few gulps and trashed that too. He cleaned his lips with a napkin and pointed to the wall behind Alfred. "See that?"

Alfred turned. His boss was pointing at the picture of a young man inside a gold frame. The man had a very big hat and a very long face. The picture seemed awfully old, and the guy vaguely familiar.

"My great-great-grandfather," his boss explained. "He was a forty-niner, a gold miner of the first hour. He broke his back digging holes in Sierra Nevada, I think. Or was it in NorCal? Anyway, at the end of the gold rush, he had so much gold he could coat himself with it. He built the foundation of my family's wealth because he knew the value of things. That trait runs in my family, and I know how to spot the same value a mile away. Now listen up. You keep up this pace and show me your will to grow, and I'll make sure your name is in front of every single face on the main floor when it's time to decide which seeds are worth watering. Do we understand each other?"

"Yes, sir."

"Good." He pointed an index finger at Alfred. "You stay with me, son, and I'll groom you into a better version of yourself. You are smooth and unused, like a raw gold nugget. You stay with me, and I'll cast you into the fire of perfection until people see you for the gold ingot you are. What do you say?"

"I thought raw gold nuggets were rough, not smooth," Alfred said without thinking.

"Whatever," his boss said dismissively. "That's beside the point."

"Of course it is, sir."

"Now get the hell out of here, and produce me results!"

Alfred left the office a bit dazed but unmistakably happy. His promotion was now closer at hand. He needed to hang on a little while longer and work harder. Just a while longer.

For the next few days, Alfred redoubled his efforts and kept waking up, going out, and getting things done. In the following weeks, he also worked on Saturdays, and he promised his boss he would continue to do so until the company's big project was completed.

Alfred welcomed the increased responsibilities. He needed them to avoid thinking too much, and so he shrouded himself with the very same things Pacific had warned him about: repetition, routine, and habits.

He woke. He went. He worked.

Then one day, something happened.

Alfred noticed that something the next morning. At first, Alfred didn't know exactly what it was. A feeling, maybe. He just knew it popped up every so often. He felt it when he was walking, browsing the Web, and reading documents.

The feeling was ubiquitous and disturbing at the same time. And there was nothing Alfred could do to silence it.

It took him several days to figure out what that feeling was, and when he did, he realized it wasn't one feeling at all but many of them blended together. There was regret in the mix, nostalgia, curiosity, and something else that felt very much like the fear of missing out.

It was a Friday night when something sparked in Alfred's mind as he walked home from work. He decided he would slightly change his routine the next day. He needed to do something different. He would once again get his Thai breakfast on Keeper Street and get to work faster by walking through the park.

And so that Saturday morning, he woke up with a feeling of anticipation and left his home longing for his favorite breakfast place.

The line of people in front of the food cart was as long as ever. When his turn came, the Thai lady smiled a very broad smile. "Long time no see you," she greeted him, her eyes shining. He placed his order. The lady handed him one khanom buang filled with extra cream.

"Yeah." Alfred took his breakfast and paid. "Been busy."

"Young man makes money," the Thai lady said approvingly while brushing her index finger with her thumb. "He buy big house. Get nice car. Then he get beautiful lady and lots of babies. Yes?"

"Maybe," Alfred said, smiling awkwardly.

"Good, good." The lady nodded. "Tomorrow, yes? See you tomorrow?"

"I think so." Alfred gave her a very generous tip and waved her goodbye.

He headed with a strange sort of anticipation toward the park. Once there, he felt his heart beating faster and faster. Alfred ran his fingers through his hair and looked around.

What was he going to do now?

He moved forward, barely conscious that his legs were bringing him closer and closer to the last place in the world he wanted to be. Only a few minutes, now, before he would see the bench surrounded by lemon trees. And maybe a man with a dark coat, smiling at him.

When Alfred got close, he hid behind a bush fewer than twenty yards away from the bench and studied the surroundings.

The bench was empty. Alfred kept looking around, but Pacific wasn't there.

Alfred gave a last look before emerging from the bush. He slumped on the bench and closed his eyes for a while.

"No freaking way," he mumbled to himself. He shook his head and exhaled slowly.

It wasn't easy to admit it, but after all he had done to avoid Pacific, there he was, alone and eager, holding his breath like a schoolboy who dreaded an exam but knew he must pass it in order to get on with his life.

What was happening to him?

He didn't know. So he just waited, and waited, until his phone's display showed him he could wait no longer.

Alfred rose from the bench and headed toward the massive building that was his workplace, knowing that he had missed out on something really important. Something he could never hope for again.

5

IN THE NAME OF FEAR

That Sunday, Alfred woke up staring blankly at the ceiling of his apartment. The alarm went off at seven thirty like it normally did. The big project his company was working on was almost complete, and every single hour counted. Every single hour, even if it was Sunday. Mr. Solidali needed him now more than ever. His promotion was at stake. He had to work harder than anyone else to get it.

And he wanted to.

Did he, though?

Of course he wanted to.

But why?

To get his own office. More money. More benefits. All of these things, he supposed.

He stared at the ceiling, asking himself questions and answering them as best he could.

And then, suddenly, Pacific's words stood up like a giant wall of fire, impossible to ignore. Those words had been on the back of Alfred's mind since they had been spoken.

"You can lose yourself in nothingness more easily than you can imagine," he repeated loudly, as if he were casting a spell. "It happens fast. When your whole life starts to look like the same old movie, the daily routine and habits make everything look stale. The repetition, the copy-and-paste of one day onto the next, are like repeated cases of déjà vu carrying you closer and closer to the grave."

Alfred finally understood why the nameless feeling had bubbled up in the first place, but it was too late now to do anything about it.

For the rest of his days, he would wake up one morning after the other and carry on with a life that had nothing to offer but predictability.

Wasn't that what he had always wanted, after all? Safety? Predictability? A stable job and a stable income?

Alfred found himself devoid of answers. He didn't know what he wanted. Not anymore.

He rose from his bed slowly, like a man heading toward a wall with a firing squad in front of it.

He got ready for work without really caring what he was doing. He didn't shave, and forgot entirely to take a shower. He put his usual clothes on and went out without bringing an umbrella, even though the sky was heavy with clouds.

Alfred's mind was numb while he walked down Main Street. He moved as if propelled by inertia. He heard the newspaper lady yelling something indistinct while waving a bunch of newspapers to the passersby. No one stopped. No one cared. The lady kept yelling and waving, yelling and waving like a marionette moved by invisible strings.

Alfred kept walking and realized his legs had brought him to Keeper Street. He waited his turn in line then asked for his usual breakfast. He heard himself say a few words, but was not sure what they were. He was just reacting to the world around him now. Nothing more, nothing less.

The Thai lady said something back to him. She looked concerned while handing him a khanom buang. Alfred was not listening. He just paid, grabbed the food in silence, and walked away.

Alfred headed toward the park without eating his breakfast, still deep in a peculiar trance. He felt lost. He felt isolated from everything and everybody.

He looked around. People moved relentlessly in every direction. He couldn't distinguish the men from the women, the tall from the short, the black from the white. All of them looked exactly the same to him. Alfred stopped in the midst of the river of people, and, for the first time since he had arrived to the city, he *really* looked at them.

Drones. Nothing more than drones powered by haste and the fear of missing out. But missing out on what, exactly? He didn't know, but the fear was a powerful fuel that kept them moving, faster and faster, day in and day out.

Alfred was powered by the very same fear; he knew that. Everybody was a slave of that condition. That was the way life was supposed to be. Anything else was off: a heresy, a joke.

He used to like jokes.

He smiled, and before he knew it, he started laughing. At first it was nothing more than a giggle, but it soon became an all-out howl.

There was no happiness in that laugh, though. It was the unexpected way his body dealt with that dreadful feeling. There was stress and confusion and emptiness, all combined to form a void like he had never experienced before.

Was he going crazy?

Someone shoved past him. Alfred lost his balance and fell.

He stayed down, his hands scratched and bloody where they had hit the asphalt. No one even glanced at him. No one could see him. They were too busy perusing the Internet with their phones, buying things they didn't need with money they didn't have. Busy moving forward. Always forward.

Alfred stood up and resumed walking.

After what felt like a thousand years, he finally got in front of the park's gate and then in front of the dreaded bench. Again, it was empty.

He stared at the bench for a very long time, completely numb, and then glanced at his phone. It was eight forty. He had to rush now if he didn't want to be late to work.

"Of course you need to go," he muttered under his breath, still looking at the bench. "You don't want to be late. Off you go, then, Alfred White. Have a painfully average day."

But he didn't go. Not this time. This time he sat on the bench and let time wash over him.

Eight forty-five.

A few minutes more, he said to himself. He needed to calm down. Just a few more minutes.

Eight forty-nine.

It would be fine. Everything would be fine.

Alfred tried to move and discovered that he couldn't. He remained seated on the bench, staring at his phone's screen. Eight forty-nine became eight fifty, and eight fifty became nine o'clock.

He was now officially late.

He had never been late.

His phone rang. It was Mr. Solidali.

He didn't answer.

The cell phone rang three more times.

He ignored it.

Alfred glanced at the passersby. It was strange to stay so still while everybody else was moving, to go against the current by doing absolutely nothing.

He looked at his phone, which was now completely blank. He could see his reflection staring back at him. Alfred thought about his life up to that point, Pacific's words always in the back of his mind.

He imagined an older version of himself. It was like looking in a mirror to the future. The older Alfred White wore the same suit, had the same job, and was holding a half-finished khanom buang in his hand. *That* Alfred had followed the plan, had lived the life he was supposed to live, and would work hard until time and routine consumed him.

That realization scared him like nothing before. It was not the kind of fear that takes you away for a few moments and accelerates your heartbeat. No. This fear was fundamentally different. It was an understanding that went deep inside him. How could he not have seen it before? He was dying. Yes, dying slowly while walking and shaving and eating and being too afraid to be late for work.

His phone rang again and again and again. He turned it off and threw it away as far as he could.

He blinked at his own boldness. That wasn't something he'd planned on doing. It just came as naturally as anything else he had ever done before.

He sat on the bench for the next hour, and for the hour after that. He felt exhausted. He lay down and closed his eyes.

It was well past noon when he woke up. He turned and saw somebody sitting next to him.

Alfred straightened himself up, rubbed his eyes, and looked at the man he never wanted to meet again yet had been desperate to find.

"Why are you here, Alfred White?" Pacific asked.

"I ..." Alfred paused. He swallowed, looked down, and finally said, "I'm not sure."

"That's a true answer," Pacific said. "I'll tell you why. You're here because you understood something today, something that scares you more than you can imagine. You are here because you have realized that you live in a prison and would do anything to escape from it."

"Yes," Alfred agreed. He wanted to add something more but didn't know exactly what, so he simply said, "I thought I'd never see you again."

"Yes. *Never.*" Pacific glanced at his broken wristwatch, the one that was never working, a small smile playing on his lips. "What a word! *Never.* We use it far too often and far too lightly. It should be handled with more care, as all such words project into the future. We should *never* forget that."

"So ..." Alfred trailed off, then looked at Pacific with deliberate attention. "Why are *you* here?"

Pacific leaned back on the bench and cast a sideways look at Alfred. "Because I see a world of unexplored possibilities sitting beside me. I know who you are, Alfred White. I know where your fear comes from, and I know why you decided long ago that the certainty of a stable life was preferable to the uncertainty of an unplanned tomorrow."

Alfred looked up at Pacific and squared his shoulders. "What makes you think you know me so well?" he asked.

"I know your past," Pacific said. "Most people are what life makes them. You are no exception. Your parents were musicians, weren't they?"

Alfred blinked, taken aback by the sudden question. "Yes," he said. "Yes, they were."

Pacific smiled knowingly. "They traveled often, and never stayed in the same place for more than a couple of years." He paused, and seemed to bathe in the confusion on Alfred's face. "They went where their music brought them and dreamed of performing on big stages with big audiences cheering them and craving their art. It never happened. They remained confined to bars and hotels, selling their music for the bare minimum to survive."

Alfred looked away. He felt uncomfortable now, like a person stripped naked and put on stage in front of a mocking audience.

"I know you slept on a couch for most of your life because your parents couldn't afford anything more than a studio apartment." Pacific paused, letting the words sink in. "I know you were unable to make friends because of your parents' lifestyle. I know they wanted you to be an artist, just like them. Yes, they wanted it real bad, didn't they? I also know your rage when you left them and swore you would never make their mistake, that you would never trade your life for the promise of a dream. You see, your past is a powerful indicator of what you have become, Alfred White. But it doesn't have to dictate the way you will be."

Alfred had to force himself to look up at the man who had proven to know him better than anyone else. "How do you know all this about me?" he asked, his voice unsteady.

Pacific waved a hand casually. "You don't really think I talk with random strangers, do you?"

"No," Alfred said after a while. "Of course not." He ran a hand over his hair. "Everything you said is true. About me, about my parents. Yes, I left them because I didn't want to end up like them. I wanted to know what would happen to me the day after tomorrow. I wanted stability."

"I understand you," Pacific said. "Art is like the icing on a cake. It's enjoyable to eat, but it doesn't feed your stomach. Your body can't run on just sugar. You pledged your allegiance to stability because it was the one thing your parents failed to provide. And you found it in the end, didn't you?"

Alfred rubbed his hands uncomfortably. "I suppose I did," he admitted.

"That is the past," Pacific said dismissively. "You're taking a step in a different direction now by sitting on this very bench, talking with me. I believe you are a young man with untapped potential. That is why I'm here with a proposition for you."

"A proposition?" Alfred's eyes narrowed. "What kind of proposition?"

"Ah." Pacific's face brightened. "I guess we could call it a period of guidance, of providing you with much sought-after answers to your questions. I will be your Virgil of course, showing you the path to the knowledge you seek."

"I don't understand."

"A mentorship," Pacific explained, standing up with a fluid motion. "That is what I'm offering you, Alfred White."

He was much taller than Alfred had expected, probably six and a half feet. Pacific walked confidently toward the nearby lemon trees and snatched one of the bitter fruits from a branch. Then he threw it to Alfred without any warning. "Catch," he said.

Alfred automatically stretched out his hands, ready to catch the lemon. But he never did. The lemon stopped in midair as though held by invisible strings. Alfred stared at the lemon, eyes wide open.

"How would you like to freeze something in the reality of its moment for as long as you please?" Pacific asked him, gesturing elaborately with his hands toward the lemon. "How would you like to live a perfect moment in your life over and over again, until the fullness of it makes you laugh and cry with joy you can barely describe? How would you like to correct a mistake before it becomes a scar deep inside your story?" Pacific paused, and the air itself seemed heavy with electricity. "Tell me, Alfred White. How would you like to witness the power of a god?"

Alfred kept staring at the impossible thing happening before him. A part of him was surprised he was not disturbed by the sight. After the déjà vu, he supposed a lemon hanging in the air was almost okay. Almost.

"How did you do it?" Alfred asked.

"Ah, there you have it." Pacific whirled on the spot. "Curiosity is bubbling inside this young mind. Should I take this question of yours as an encouraging nod to my mentorship proposition?"

Alfred found himself smiling.

"Very well," Pacific said. "An answer for a question, then. How did I do it, you ask me. I used time as a currency, that is how."

"A currency?"

"When you fancy something, say, a pair of shoes"—Pacific pointed to Alfred's shoes—"you must be willing to pay for it. Time is no different. If you want time, you must be ready to pay with time to get it."

"That doesn't make any sense."

"Precisely," Pacific agreed earnestly. "That is why a mentorship is needed. To make sense of what seems senseless. You follow me?"

"Not really."

"Very good." Pacific made a casual move with his fingers, and the lemon was back in his hand.

"Unbelievable," Alfred mumbled.

"It was, before the lemon stopped and came back to my hand," Pacific pointed out. "Now it is just a part of your knowledge. Catch."

Alfred was too late to catch the lemon.

"So." Pacific sat back on the bench. "Do you want to explore the subject further?"

Alfred picked up the lemon from the ground. He weighed it in his hand for a few seconds. "Yes, I would like it very much."

"Let's make a deal, then," Pacific said brightly. "You will be my protégé tomorrow. You will shadow me and get to know what I do and why." He raised a hand before Alfred could speak. "But listen carefully. In exchange for my patronage, you will follow my instructions, even though they might seem odd, and will not interfere with my decisions. What do you say?"

Alfred looked around uncomfortably. "To be honest, it feels a bit loose and broad. I mean, how do you expect me to make a decision based on ... not knowing anything?"

"A leap of faith is always risky." Pacific shrugged nonchalantly. "The fear of the unknown is what weeds out those unworthy of continuing the journey. However, I understand not everyone is ready for it. If that's the case, I bid you farewell." Pacific started rising.

"Wait!" Alfred grabbed Pacific's coat. The last thing he wanted was to lose, again, his chance to get answers. "I'm in!" he blurted. "I'll do it!"

Pacific looked at Alfred for a long while. "Very well," he said, sitting back beside Alfred. He took the glove off his right hand. "Let's shake on it, then."

Alfred studied the man's long fingers. They were slender, and more white than pink.

Pacific spat on his palm and stretched out his hand. Alfred winced.

"Well?" Pacific said, waiting.

Alfred looked hesitant. "Do I have to spit on my hand?" he asked.

"You most certainly do."

The young man sighed. He spat on his palm, and the two shook hands.

Something odd happened then. Alfred looked at their clasped hands and then at the man in front of him. It was as if a veil of smoke had thinned, and he could see Pacific more clearly. Pacific wasn't a stranger anymore. He was a man who had bound himself to a promise. He didn't quite know why he was so certain of it. It was a peculiar feeling he could not explain, like knowing you were surrounded by water even though you could not see it. He knew, inwardly, that Pacific could not deny him the knowledge he had promised.

"It's done." Pacific smiled broadly, showing for the first time a raw set of white teeth. "You're mine tomorrow."

"Yes," Alfred agreed, nodding awkwardly while looking at Pacific. "Tomorrow. Yes. For sure."

"Well now." Pacific looked at the gray sky. "I've a few things to prepare before tomorrow's cathartic journey. We'll meet up in front of your favorite breakfast place at eleven. Sharp. We'll have a tight schedule to follow. Oh, yes ..." He took something else from his pocket. "You will still need this." He handed Alfred his cell phone. "Remember? Time's a trickster. Reign over it, or be reigned over by it."

And, that said, Pacific stood and walked away, whistling joyfully.

SIX FEET ABOVE

Alfred White snapped awake at the sound of a car horn. He looked around, his heart racing. The room was filled with light from the half-opened window. He squeezed his eyes shut, rubbed them hard, and looked around again.

What time was it? His bleary eyes set upon the bedside table, where he found his cell phone. He touched the screen and the device lit up.

It was just a few minutes before ten. Alfred stared at the numbers in disbelief. Ten. He had never slept that late since ... Well, he had never slept that late. Period.

What happened to the alarm? Had he forgotten to set it the day before?

Alfred didn't waste time on those questions. He jumped out of bed, rushed toward the bathroom, stumbled on a shoe, and fell hard on his back. He dropped the phone, too.

"Shit," he groaned. He rose slowly, looking for his phone while still trying to understand what had happened. If he called Mr. Solidali now, he might still be able to explain why he was not—

His phone's alarm rang. Alfred frowned at it. He had set it to go off that late? Why?

And then, he suddenly remembered everything.

He had no job to go to. He had decided to stay on that bench the day before, and to ignore Mr. Solidali's calls. That meant he'd quit. Plain and simple.

Alfred slumped to the floor, now fully awake.

He stayed there, completely still, a legion of thoughts storming inside his head.

He reached out to his phone, turned off the alarm, and looked at the screen.

There were five unanswered calls from Mr. Solidali, and two messages in his inbox. They were from his boss. Alfred bit his lips. Doubt crept up in the form of regret. The day before he had literally thrown away months of effort—his whole damn life—for what, exactly?

Everything had seemed so clear in the moment: at the park, sitting on that bench, brooding about his life. But now it was muddy at best.

A part of him started second-guessing what he had done. If he called Mr. Solidali now and made up some kind of believable excuse, would his project coordinator believe him?

But why would Alfred do that? He didn't want his job back. He had made a decision and intended to stick to it until the end. He would not go back to his old life. He would find out who the man called Pacific really was, and from there ... Well, he would figure it out.

Alfred breathed in and exhaled slowly. He erased all the messages without reading them and placed the cell phone back on the bedside table. He looked around, a bit lost. Now that his routine was broken, he felt disorganized and unsettled.

He was jobless. He was free. He was completely and utterly mad.

Alfred rose from the floor awkwardly, feeling stunned.

It dawned on him only then that he had an appointment with Pacific.

Alfred went to the bathroom, shaved out of habit, and took a quick shower. In front of his wardrobe, he moved away from the shirts and the trousers and instead grabbed a simple blue hoodie and a pair of jeans.

He took his keys and went outside with zero ideas about what to expect from his day.

~

He was surprised at the brightness outside. A cloudless sky reigned over everything. Alfred looked up with the same amazement one might manifest when looking at an aurora. The past few weeks he had grown accustomed to the rain and the cold. After all, he had seen little else since he had moved to the city.

He started walking down Main Street without haste. The usual stream of businesspeople that packed the sidewalks in the early morning were nowhere to be found. In their stead were mostly very young or very old people, enjoying the day's sun.

By the time Alfred turned onto Keeper Street, it was around lunchtime. There was an even longer line of people waiting.

Alfred watched as the Thai lady served a customer then looked around, excused herself with a quick gesture, and disappeared into the back of the truck.

"The smell of the morning is in the air, and the sky is crisp blue."

Alfred turned toward the familiar voice. Pacific was walking with a confident stride toward him, wearing his usual dark outfit.

"A magnificent day to start over, don't you think?" Pacific pointed at the line of people. "There's quite a few of them, mm-hm?" he said.

"Yeah." Alfred nodded. "You want to get something to eat?"

"Indeed."

"In that case, it looks like we're going to wait for a while."

"Nonsense. We're going to get our lunch at once. But before that, take this."

Pacific handed him a camera with a strap attached to it. Alfred took it awkwardly. The camera was big and bulky, but incredibly light for its size. "What's this?" he asked.

"That, my young friend, is a DSLR camera." Pacific touched the lens cap. "Light travels through this lens, to a mirror that sends the image to either the viewfinder or the image sensor. That's how we get pictures in this marvelous age of gadgets and technology."

Alfred frowned. "I know what a camera is, thank you very much. What do you want me to do with it?"

"You'll be taking some pictures today."

"Really?" Alfred weighed up the camera. He seemed doubtful. "Okay, but just so you know, I'm not very good with these sorts of things. I mean, I can take decent pictures with my phone, but that's as far as my photography skills go."

"It's really simple. Look." Pacific took back the camera and showed him how to handle it. "You aim, zoom, press the button halfway, and then press it all the way. Just like this. See? Piece of cake. Now listen up. When I say so, start taking pictures of the truck."

"The truck?" Alfred asked. "You mean the—"

But Pacific wasn't listening anymore. He moved away from Alfred and toward the last man waiting in line, a bald, short fellow with a stomach so vast, he surely didn't need another khanom buang.

Alfred followed Pacific awkwardly, wondering what was going to happen.

"Excuse me, sir." Pacific touched the man's shoulder to get his attention. "Is *this* the famous Thai vendor of Keeper Street?"

"I think so," the fat man said, shrugging. "It's the only one around as far as I know."

Pacific nodded briskly and turned toward Alfred. With a voice loud enough to be heard by anyone around, he said, "That's it! This is the place! The poor man was brought to the hospital after eating here! Take a good angle of the cart, and a panoramic view of the street. What are you waiting for? Action!"

Alfred jerked to attention and started taking pictures, aiming and shooting.

"Excuse me," a woman a few places away in the queue said, looking at Pacific. "Did you say *hospital*?"

"Indeed." Pacific nodded gravely. Then, turning toward Alfred, he said, "Don't forget the inside of the truck! Take some more! Quickly, now. She's still in the back. She won't notice."

"A man, you said?" Another person joined the conversation. "He went to the hospital after eating here?"

"Yes and yes," Pacific answered, while people broke the line and crowded around him. "A man was sent to the hospital after eating a khanom buang sold at this very place." He pointed to the food cart. "A severe case of strombolocktosis, it is assumed by the doctors. The poor fellow will be in bed for a full week and won't be able to digest anything other than liquids for much longer than that."

An ever-increasing murmur spread like wildfire.

"Good Lord," said the woman who had first spoken. "Honey, let's get out of here!" She pulled her husband with her and led the way out of Keeper Street.

The rest of the people soon followed her, and by the time Alfred had shot the last picture, he and Pacific were the only ones left.

"You can stop taking pictures now."

"What the hell is strombolocktosis?" Alfred asked, turning the camera off.

"I have no idea." Pacific shrugged. "But the word is long enough and sounds scary enough."

"What?" Alfred blurted. "You lied to them?"

"Lied?" Pacific frowned. "I prefer to say I manufactured reality to my advantage, but you're more than welcome to use that word if it suits you."

"I can't believe it," Alfred said, eyeing Pacific with disdain. "People will steer clear of this place now that you've spread the rumor. Nobody will buy from her again."

"Life is an unfair ride on the back of a reckless bull, my young friend."

"That is not funny."

"Oh, I see it now." Pacific glanced at the food cart with a knowing smile. "You seem to be personally invested in the lady that sells you sugar. Mm-hm? That is cute. Now open your ears and close you heart. It's wisdom time. Lies are cheap and abundant. Time, on the other hand, is a scarce resource, difficult to get. If a lie can buy me time, I won't hesitate a second to use it. Capisce?"

Alfred was not happy with the answer, but before he could say anything else, the Thai lady returned from the back of the truck. She looked around, searching for people who were no longer there.

"Where is everybody?" she said.

Pacific stepped forward and smiled a broad smile. "We'll take two of your finest khanom buang, ma'am," he said.

The Thai lady didn't seem to notice Pacific's request. She was still looking for her customers.

"Well?" Pacific snapped a finger and finally got the lady's attention. "The clock is ticking."

The woman said something in Thai while glancing around one last time. Then she busied herself with the big spoon she used to stir the cream and put it on the crepes, and in less than two minutes she had the food ready for them.

Pacific took one crepe, handed the other to Alfred, and walked away, leaving Alfred to pay. Alfred handed the lady a ten-dollar bill. Then, because he felt bad for her, he switched the ten-dollar bill with a twenty.

The Thai lady waved her hands wildly. "That is way too mu—"

"No, it's not," Alfred said resolutely. "Please take it. And ... good luck."

Alfred caught up with Pacific, who had walked almost all the way back to Main Street. "You're welcome, by the way," Alfred said sarcastically.

Pacific licked the cream off his lips. "Beg your pardon?"

"The crepe? My money? You're welcome."

"Oh, this?" Pacific looked at his lunch. He took another bite. "I always forget to pay for this kind of stuff."

"That makes you a thief. You know that, right?"

"Hardly. I just know the fair price of things that don't have one."

"Well, the *fair* price of the crepe you're wolfing down is four dollars and fifty cents, just so you know."

"I sense annoyance," Pacific said, studying Alfred's gloomy expression. "Is money an issue?"

"No, it's not," Alfred said quickly. He grimaced and added, "I mean, I'm not a money-making machine, plus I'm now jobless and ... well ... that's not really the point I was trying to make. Anyway, where are we going?"

They walked a while longer on Main Street before turning down a narrow, dark lane with patches of fresh asphalt here and there.

"We have two meetings today," Pacific declared. "Both will help *you* broaden your world and *me* understand a few more things about you."

"Meetings?" Alfred asked, puzzled. "With whom?"

"Some call it Destiny, others Moira." Pacific raised both hands as if mimicking a weight scale. "The name doesn't really matter, only the outcome it brings people."

"Okay." Alfred rolled his eyes. "What does that mean in plain English?"

"You'll find out soon enough. Here we are."

Alfred looked around. They had reached the very end of the street. There was nothing around except some parked cars, a broken fountain, and a convenience store.

"There's nothing here," Alfred said, looking at the store, "unless you fancy a cheap hot dog and undercooked fries."

"See in front of the store?" Pacific pointed a few feet away from the entrance. "The Enterprise parked right there?"

Alfred followed Pacific's finger. Less than thirty yards away, there was a very expensive sports car. It was painted silver and looked like a spaceship.

"Yeah," Alfred said. "I see it."

Just then the store's door opened, and a chubby middle-aged man wearing a bright blue suit came out. He walked toward the sports car and placed a paper bag on the hood, rummaging inside the bag until he found a gigantic cheeseburger and a can of soda.

"See that fellow?" Pacific asked, pointing.

"Yes, I do." Alfred watched the fat man take a huge bite of the cheeseburger.

"Allow me to introduce you to Mr. Steve Rowsons Junior," Pacific said, waving his hands in an elaborate, introductory gesture. "He's forty-nine years old and was born in Atlanta, Georgia. He's divorced, with two kids who haven't seen him in a decade. He works as a financial adviser at the prestigious Thur'as & Sons Capital Group Limited, makes six figures per year, and hates his job. Yes. That should be enough to give you an insight into his life."

Alfred frowned. "How do you know all that stuff about him?"

"I do my homework and ask the right questions to the right people."

"I still don't understand why we are looking at him."

"I'm not looking at him." Pacific lifted his chin slightly. "I'm looking *above* him."

"Above?" Alfred looked above Steve's head. "What do you mean? There's nothing above him."

"For now." Pacific looked at Alfred. "Now listen. Think of what I said about that man. Think of his name, his age, his place of birth. Think of his profession. Then, while you're doing it, picture a square in your mind. It can be any square of any color and size you want."

Alfred's eyebrows shot up. "A square?"

"A quadrilateral with four equal sides and four equal angles."

"I know what a square is. Look, I don't get what you're trying to—"

"I should have mentioned this earlier," Pacific said, raising a hand to interrupt Alfred. "This is not question time. You will follow my instructions, even though they might seem odd. You agreed on that, remember?"

"Yes, I remember," Alfred said resignedly. "What do you want me to do again?"

"Just look above his head—six feet above his head, to be exact. Think of what I said about that man, and picture a square."

Alfred shook his head. He looked at the man still eating his cheeseburger, and he looked at Pacific. "Can I just say this sounds very weird? I mean, I don't mind—"

"I know it sounds odd. Just do it."

Alfred was skeptical but did as he was told. He looked above Steve's head and tried to picture the image of a square while thinking of what Pacific had said about Steve.

One minute passed. Two minutes. Alfred felt really stupid staring at nothing.

"Look, I don't get it," Alfred finally said, giving up. "What do you want me to see? Hm? There is absolutely nothing there, only air!"

"You're not thinking," Pacific warned him. "I can feel it. You're just wondering why you should do something that makes you look stupid. You want knowledge? Then be ready to accept it. Stop focusing on yourself. Concentrate. Remember to picture a square while you're looking above him."

"I just don't—"

"Stop trying to rationalize everything, young man. There's nothing logical in my request. Nothing. I'm asking you to step out of your comfort zone and to trust me. Can you do it or not?"

Alfred rubbed the back of his neck. "Okay. Fine," he said. "I'll do it." He noticed Pacific's grave expression. "Seriously this time. I promise. Picture a square. Look six feet above his head. Think about his life. Got it. On it."

Alfred closed his eyes and concentrated on forming the image of a square in his mind. It took him some time, but in the end he could see it. It was as big as a human torso, and silver like Steve's car.

When Alfred opened his eyes again, he had the imaginary square still sharp in his mind.

He looked at Steve and recalled what Pacific had said about him.

Middle aged.

Divorced.

Two children.

Prestigious.

Wealthy.

Unhappy.

Something flashed above Steve's head for a fraction of a second. It was no more than a spark of light that disappeared before Alfred could be sure it had ever existed.

The young man blinked several times in disbelief. He looked at Pacific, his mouth half-opened.

"Don't look at me," Pacific said, pointing at Steve. "Look at your man."

Alfred obeyed. Again he pictured the square in his mind, and again he thought about the man's life.

"Good." Pacific nodded. "Keep looking. Concentrate on his story, on his life, and visualize the image of a square in your mind. Evoke it, seize it, and use it to see."

Alfred did it. The second time was easier than the first. Again the spark of light flashed and disappeared almost immediately. Then appeared again. Alfred kept staring at the spot where the light had appeared, six feet above Steve's head, putting all his effort into the task, concentrating on keeping the image of the silver square sharp in his mind. Finally, he was able to see it for more than a moment.

The spark of light became a stable streak of light that settled into a defined shape. Alfred's eyes widened when he understood what it was. It was a number—a red number, or rather a series of numbers. There was a two, followed by the number forty-four. No. Forty-three. Forty-two ... forty-one ... forty. Every second, the number decreased.

It was a countdown.

"What in the name of Jesus is that?" Alfred gasped.

"What do you see?" Pacific stared at him with anticipation.

"I see numbers," Alfred said, still stunned. "A countdown, I think. Two minutes and fifteen seconds. Fourteen, now."

"Well done." Pacific nodded approvingly. "That, young man, is Steve's remaining life span."

Alfred jerked his head toward Pacific. "What?"

"You heard me. That is how long Steve has left to live. Just over two minutes."

"Are you serious?"

"I am. Now gather yourself." Pacific pointed to the camera Alfred was holding. "Take a good picture of him."

"A picture?"

"Yes, a picture."

"You mean—"

"Take a picture of that man," Pacific ordered. "And be quick about it. We don't have much time left."

"Okay." Alfred aimed, zoomed, and took a couple of pictures.

"Let me see." Pacific snatched the camera from his hands. They both looked at the picture's preview.

The pictures were sharp. The numbers were there, too, clearly visible above Steve's head.

"That's good enough," Pacific said, looking pleased.

Alfred licked his lips. "Are those numbers real?" he asked, glancing at the countdown and still debating its reality. "I mean, the pictures show them, right?"

"This camera is special," Pacific explained, patting the camera's body. "If you were to take a picture of that man with anything else, you would see nothing. A normal camera freezes a moment in time. This one freezes time itself."

Alfred had no idea what the hell that meant. He looked back at Steve and realized the countdown was almost up.

"It's go time," Pacific said, pushing back his sunglasses. "Twelve ... eleven ... ten ..."

Steve suddenly yelped, and dropped his cheeseburger on the ground.

"What's happening?" Alfred asked, astonished.

Steve grabbed his chest with both hands and started howling in pain as he fell on his knees.

"Oh my God," Alfred said, both hands over his mouth. "He's ... he's having a heart attack or something." He looked at Pacific with expectantly. "We gotta do something!"

"We're doing something," Pacific said, his arms crossed. "We're watching him die."

Alfred could not believe what was happening.

He moved a couple of steps forward. He didn't know what to do, but he needed to do something.

Seven ...

Steve screamed in pain, a high-pitched stream of blurted words, begging for help. Alfred ran toward him.

Four ...

Alfred got to him. Steve's eyes were filled with horror.

"It's okay, buddy," Alfred assured him, looking around frantically. "Hang on. I'll ... I'll get somebody to help. I ... I ..."

One ...

Pacific clapped his hands, and the countdown disappeared.

Steve stopped moving. His eyes were still open, but there was nothing beyond them, only blankness. Only death.

Alfred ran his fingers through his hair. "Oh my God," he murmured. "This is not ... This is not happening."

He placed his ear to Steve's chest. There was no heartbeat.

"No, no, no," Alfred muttered. He started shaking Steve's body. "Come on, buddy! Come on!"

He needed to do something. Mouth-to-mouth resuscitation, maybe? But how? He had no idea how.

His phone! He could call somebody. An ambulance. Yes. Alfred took his phone out of his pocket, but his hands were shaking so hard he dropped it. He could not move, he could not see clearly, he could hardly breathe. His gaze returned to Steve's horrified, wide eyes. Alfred's head spun. He coughed, and his chest felt heavy. He was going to be sick.

"Breathe." He heard Pacific's voice behind him. "It's just a corpse. Can't do you any harm."

Alfred swallowed. He left Steve's body, which slumped to the ground. "I ... think I'm going to be sick."

Pacific sighed. "If you must," he said.

Alfred could do nothing more than bend and puke right there.

"And there goes your lunch," Pacific said, his hands resting on his hips. "What's the matter? Can't stomach death?"

"I've never seen—" Alfred cut himself off. He was fighting for air. The world kept spinning around him. He managed to sit on the ground, and took some seconds to gather himself. "I've never seen somebody ... die."

Pacific clasped his hands behind his back. "I see somebody die most days."

Silence stretched between them. The street was still empty. Nobody seemed to have heard Steve's screams. Nobody had come out of the convenience store.

"We need to call an ambulance," Alfred said, wiping his mouth with the back of his hand.

"What for?" Pacific asked.

"I ... I don't know." Alfred was gasping for air. "They could try to revive him, or something."

Pacific shook his head definitively. He bent over Steve's body and, looking at the man's blank eyes, said, "He has passed that point. He's never coming back."

Pacific took off his sunglasses, and for the first time Alfred could see the color of his eyes. They were a deep gray that reminded him of cold stone. A thin, red rim surrounded his pupils, separating them clearly from the gray irises.

"You did well," Pacific said, glancing at Alfred. "I didn't expect you to see much your first time." He turned on his camera and took a picture of Steve's body up close.

Alfred looked at Pacific, and what he saw made him shiver. There was nothing on the man's face. No sorrow, no excitement, no worry, no delight over the man's death. No emotion at all. Pacific reminded him of a businessperson talking about last quarter's earnings.

It did seem like Pacific was used to seeing people die. What kind of person saw death on a daily basis?

Now that Alfred's mind was clearing, it became clear to him that Pacific had known Steve was about to die.

Pacific stepped away from Steve and offered Alfred his hand. "Can you stand?" he asked.

"I think so."

"Here. Let me help you."

Alfred took his hand, and Pacific helped him up.

"Now look at me." Pacific said. "You need to calm down. Breathe in, and breathe out. Yes, just like that. Now do it again."

Alfred did. After a while, he felt a bit better.

"Sit here." Pacific pointed to the hood of Steve's car. Alfred dragged his feet and sat. Pacific rummaged inside his pocket and emerged with a small, round object. "Eat this," he said.

"What is it?"

"A candy. Caramel flavor."

"I don't want it," Alfred closed his eyes and waved the candy away. The thought of food made him sick again.

"You do want it," Pacific insisted, pushing the candy to Alfred's hand. "This is a special candy. It will help you feel better. Trust me."

"What do you mean by *special*?"

"Just eat it. You'll feel better. I promise."

Alfred clenched his jaw but didn't argue. He had no strength for it. He unwrapped the candy and ate it.

Alfred felt an inexplicable wave of heat as soon as he swallowed the candy. It felt strange but invigorating, like drinking a mug of hot chocolate in the middle of winter. His muscles relaxed instantly.

"How do you feel now?" Pacific asked.

"I ... I feel better, actually. Much better."

"Glad to hear it."

A crow came down from the sky and landed on Steve's stomach. It stayed on top of it for a while then scampered toward the half-finished burger and started picking at it. Another two crows soon followed the first one, joining the feast.

"Is he really dead?" Alfred asked, trying not to stare at Steve's face.

"As dead as it gets."

Alfred had a million more questions and no way to ask them. He felt devoid of everything, numb and confused. He didn't remember the last time he had felt so lost and scared.

"Come on," Pacific said, gesturing for him to stand. "Steve is going to attract attention soon enough, and we want to be far away before that happens. Besides, we've got another appointment with Destiny, remember?"

The tall man turned and walked away from the corpse.

Alfred looked over Steve's horrified expression one last time then stood awkwardly and staggered behind Pacific.

7

THE RICHEST PLACE IN THE WORLD

They walked a couple of blocks in silence, Pacific leading the way and Alfred slightly behind, deep in thought.

Alfred glanced at Pacific. The tall man was whistling joyfully. Alfred looked away. Whistling! A person had just died in front of their eyes, and he was whistling! It was so wrong it wasn't even funny.

Alfred wiped the sweat from his forehead and tried to calm down. He needed to analyze what had happened.

The fact that Pacific knew when Steve was going to die, the appearance of the countdown, the camera immortalizing the event and showing the red numbers. All of that had no right to be.

For this reason Alfred looked for answers outside the realm of reality, to what society labeled inexplicable, impossible, and completely, utterly mad.

Magic was the answer that came to him first: dark magic, like sorcery, the stuff of fantasy books and fairy tales.

The thought made him shiver. Here he was, an adult person thinking of wizards and fairy tales to make sense to what had happened.

Of course he didn't believe that kind of stuff. His mind wasn't going to accept the inexplicable. It was going to fight it, to constrain those events to something familiar, something Alfred understood. But it was a useless effort.

You can't explain magic when it happens, he found himself thinking. *You either believe it or you don't.*

Again Alfred looked at Pacific. This time he studied his lean figure in the raincoat. He tried to unveil the mystery behind the person who had come into his life so suddenly. The sunglasses once again shielded Pacific's gray eyes, and the beanie he always wore covered his forehead and ears. The only portion of visible skin was the lower part of his face, clean shaven and as pale as a hospital wall. Had that man something to hide?

Alfred looked at Pacific for so long that it became staring.

Other questions surfaced like bubbles in the pond of his mind.

Who was this person? Why had they met? How could he possibly know when people were going to die?

"Are you the Devil?" Alfred heard himself uttering the question, but couldn't believe he'd actually asked it. It had been a passing thought, no more than a glimpse of awareness at the back of his mind. But the question was there now, in the real world, and Alfred could not take it back. So he waited, and hoped the answer would not be the one he feared.

A wry smile flashed on Pacific's face. "The Devil is an idea made up of stories and faith," he said. "I'm flesh and bones. There is no Devil without Christianity, there is no story without a storyteller."

"I don't understand."

"I am a fact of life," Pacific explained. "Think of it this way: if you were to erase every single religion from the history of mankind, I would still be standing in front of you. No, Alfred White. I'm not the Devil. I'm just a fellow trying to make ends meet."

Alfred didn't know if he could trust Pacific's answer. However, a part of him suspected that if the Devil really existed, he would probably answer that question the same way.

"But you can see when somebody is going to die," Alfred pointed out.

"I can," Pacific agreed, "but so can you. Does that make us the Devil?"

"No, it doesn't." Alfred thought a bit about that. "I could see the countdown, yes, but why? Because I was with you? Maybe because you did something special to me and—"

"There's nothing special in seeing those numbers," Pacific said, cutting him off. "I'm not special because I can see death coming, my young friend. I'm special because I can use that knowledge to my advantage."

"What do you mean?"

"Understand this: death is a commodity, a resource that can be used," Pacific said. "That is the main reason why I'm here. I'm here because I can use death and what it brings with it."

Alfred was very confused. "That doesn't make any sense. How can death be a commodity? Death is just death. The cessation of life. The end."

"That is true for a person who can't see anything beyond that point. But trust me when I say, there is much more than simply an *end* for somebody who understands that death is only one part of a bigger truth. When you are able to see death as a commodity, it becomes a story, just like money. And a story can be a good one or a bad one. It depends very much on the person who's telling it, and on who's listening."

"I don't understand what you're trying to say. It just doesn't make any sense!"

"What, precisely, is puzzling you?"

"Um. *Everything!*"

"Well, you'll have to be a bit more specific than that if you want a meaningful answer."

Alfred sighed. "Okay, let me get this straight. Basically, you just know a bunch of random stuff about a person, picture a square in your mind, and you can see his or her remaining life span? Is that how it works?"

"No." Pacific shook his head. "It's not random stuff, it's information that makes up that person's life. And thinking of a square only works for men. You need to picture a circle if you want it to work for women."

"Why a circle?"

"Because the circle is the perfect shape," Pacific said with a knowing smile.

"Oh." Alfred had no idea what that meant, but he also had no idea how to explore the subject further. "I ... I don't know what else to say," he admitted.

"Then say nothing," Pacific suggested. "Don't be in such a rush to understand. To figure things out. The path to knowledge is a marathon, not a sprint. Watch, and learn. Words can bring you only so far. Experience is a far better teacher."

"What is that supposed to mean?"

"It means that knowledge is a double-edged knife. You have to be trained to handle it without hurting yourself. I always choose words carefully when talking to you because I'm aware that the wrong word in the wrong place could crush you and cast your sanity into oblivion. You are not ready for the knowledge you seek, Alfred White. Not yet."

Alfred muttered under his breath but said nothing more.

Pacific turned left then right. Alfred followed him to a part of the city he had never been before. They walked for a few minutes along a commercial street with lots of stores and street vendors. Eventually the stores became scanter, and they found themselves in a quiet neighborhood on the edge of the West End. It was a residential district, with cars parked along the street but almost no stores.

In the middle of the neighborhood there was a massive building of gray marble that stood out in the jungle of houses. It was beautiful and imposing and seemed quite old. A white cross as big as a tree dominated the entire structure.

Around the building, a metal fence spanned from left to right as far as the eye could see.

"Speaking of the Devil," Pacific said, looking at the white cross with a smirk. "Here we are. Our second meeting with Destiny is about to begin."

"A church?" Alfred asked, taken aback. "You want to go inside that church?"

"We're not going inside it," Pacific corrected him. "We're going *behind* it." Pacific walked past the gate, and so did Alfred.

The church was not the only building inside the fence, only the biggest one. There was also a smaller building that looked like a chapel, an apartment unit, and a parking lot covered by solar panels.

Alfred didn't see a living soul on the property, but he heard sounds and voices coming from inside the church. People were praying and singing. Apparently, there was a mass going on.

They walked past a line of trees that flanked a small garden with statues of angels and a couple of small fountains. A few steps beyond the fountains, the garden ended, and they reached the limit of the church's massive structure. Alfred looked in front of him, where there was nothing except a very large and very empty square. It was plain and bare, surrounded by the same enclosure that protected the entire property.

This was a graveyard, and a very big one at that. Alfred had no idea there was one so vast inside the city.

Hundreds of rectangular shapes stuck out of the ground like the white, gray, and black fingers of a multitude of buried giants trying to emerge from the ground.

"The richest place in the world." Pacific looked around, arms spread wide as if he owned the entire place. "As author Les Brown poetically put it, 'Where you will find all the hopes and dreams that were never fulfilled, the books that were never written, the songs that were never sung, the inventions that were never shared, the cures that were never discovered, all because someone was too afraid to take that first step, keep with the problem, or determined to carry out their dream.' " Pacific looked at Alfred and smiled his half smile. "Don't you find it a fitting quote?"

"Why are we in a graveyard?"

"Mr. Steve Rowsons Junior will be buried here," Pacific explained. He pointed to a bunch of tombstones a few yards away. "His parents are waiting for him six feet below the ground."

"You mean *that* man?"

Pacific nodded. "I wonder what he saw in the last moments of his life, when he knew he was going to die? Were they the things he regretted doing? The things he didn't do? The dreams he never pursued?" Pacific paused. He looked at the closest tombstone a few steps away and said, "He had a dream when he was younger, you know? Steve wanted to be an artist. A painter, to be precise. Oh, he wanted it so bad! He would wake up in the middle of the night with an idea, an image in his mind, and he would take a canvas and paint with passion for hours. He would pour himself in those paintings, and he would look at them with satisfaction and pride because he would see himself in them." Pacific started walking toward the nearest tombstone. Alfred followed him.

"His family told him he had no chance." Pacific stopped in front of the tombstone. "His friends laughed at him when he confessed his passion. There was no future in his dream, they told him. No career, no money to be made. And somewhere along the way, Steve listened. He listened, and he changed. He decided his dream was too unrealistic, too childish. He decided to live a life other people had chosen for him. And so he went to finance school, got his degree, found a stable job, married a woman he never really loved, fathered two children he never really wanted, and lived unhappily ever after."

Pacific took the glove off his right hand and touched the surface of the tombstone. In fact, he wasn't simply touching it—he was caressing it. One slow, gentle stroke after the other.

"What are you trying to say?" Alfred took a step forward. He, too, was looking at the tombstone now. "That he would have been better off as a penniless bastard at the side of a street, selling paintings? You were the one who said art is just the icing on a cake."

"That is my take on it," Pacific said. "Not Steve's. Do you understand the difference?"

"Not really."

"I'm not Steve," Pacific explained. "I didn't live his life. But I guess this is all pointless now. There is no right or wrong answer when it comes to the end of a person's journey. It's like looking at footprints on a beach; the first wave on the sand wipes them out of existence. They might have never been there at all. Steve's desire has turned into those footprints. It's reduced to the shadow of a past that belongs to oblivion."

"What is that supposed to mean?"

"It means that is easy to judge a person when the corpse is cold and forgotten." Pacific placed both hands on the tombstone, resting his weight on it. "Only a fool judges an apple when it is already rotten. I am but an observer of death and of all things that may have happened and didn't. Tell me, Alfred White. Did you ever have a dream?"

Alfred blinked, surprised by the question. "What?" he asked.

"A dream," Pacific repeated. "Have you ever had one?"

The image of a young boy with a cowboy hat, holding a whip and following maps with a big, fat, red cross on it flashed before Alfred's eyes. The memory came to him so naturally he couldn't believe it was his.

"Well?" Pacific looked at him expectantly.

Alfred shifted uncomfortably. He looked bashful.

"I know you're thinking something," Pacific teased. "Don't be shy, now. Set the thought free."

Alfred's reluctance was plain, but eventually he nodded. "Well, now that you mention it, when I was ten I wanted to be a treasure hunter. I wanted to explore exotic places, solve riddles, and find impossibly precious treasure I would sell to museums for glory and fame. You know, like Indiana Jones."

"Yes," Pacific said. "I get the picture. What stopped you?"

"What do you mean?"

"What stopped you from becoming Indiana Jones?"

Alfred blinked, lost. Was that a serious question?

"Well?" Pacific pressed him. "What stopped you?"

"I don't know." Alfred said defensively. "It was just a bunch of movies, I guess. Just a young boy's fancy."

"That's not true, and you know it." Pacific took off his sunglasses, his gray eyes fixed on Alfred. "I'll ask you once more. What stopped you from becoming Indiana Jones?"

Alfred didn't answer. He had no idea what Pacific wanted him to say.

The tall man looked at the tombstone one last time then put his glove and sunglasses back on. "When you have an answer to that question," he said, "you'll have figured out what most people never will." Pacific looked around, taking everything in. "This place you call a graveyard is a museum of lost things, broken and neglected. It is full of countless Steves, men and women who died without realizing their full potential, bringing to the grave their true selves. It's sad, but it's also how things work in the world you live in, the world of commitments, of haste, of denial and delusion."

Alfred followed Pacific's gaze, and for the first time he really looked at the graveyard. There were bodies here, dead people rotting beneath their feet. Alfred understood what Pacific was saying. In a way, he could even relate to it. Very few of the people he knew considered themselves happy or fulfilled. His coworkers at the Spear were good examples of that. Most of them were always complaining and doing nothing to change. They were unwilling to change themselves and their circumstances. But time was the constant that united them all. In the end, they all ended up there. Broken things, Pacific had said. Broken and neglected. Dead things.

Pacific turned to Alfred. "Think of what you saw here as the first lesson I will teach you, the first piece of knowledge I will give you. Every choice people make has a consequence in the book of their life. They can write on that book, but they can't change what's written. At best, they can tear off pages. And that is what Steve did for most of his life. He wrote stories on that book and tore pages apart every single day of his adult life."

Pacific's words were difficult to decipher, but they made sense in a peculiar sort of way. Alfred just needed to figure out how. And for that, he was going to need time. He knew that now.

Pacific zoomed in with his camera and took one picture of the graveyard. He looked at the picture's preview, nodded in satisfaction, then looked back at Alfred. "So far I showed you a glimpse of the truth you want to unveil. You don't understand it, and will never fully understand it if you're not willing to make sacrifices. Now listen carefully. This is at the very core of the mentorship I've offered you. Sacrifices must be the bedrock of your knowledge. Without sacrifices, this journey means nothing."

Alfred looked at him, puzzled. "What do you mean? What kind of sacrifices?"

Pacific tapped Alfred's forehead with his index finger. "Your curiosity is a powerful engine for change, but it will never be enough if it's not propelled by the will to sacrifice what you are now for the promise of what you might became. You're still trapped in the same world of fear that killed Steve. I can teach you how to free yourself from that fear, but you'll have to trust me. Now it is time for you to make a choice, and you must understand the importance of it. When we shook hands yesterday, we made an agreement that we are both bound to. You agreed to give me one day of your life so that you could witness the truth behind my existence, and I agreed to give you the knowledge you seek by the time the sun set. After what you saw, a part of you wants to bail out. I can feel it. That is understandable. You saw a person die, and it shook you deeply. The part of you that never wanted to meet me, now wants to walk away from this commitment." Pacific took two steps toward Alfred. "I'm giving you the chance right here, right now. Say that you forsake your commitment, and I'll release you from it."

As Pacific stepped toward him, Alfred unconsciously took two steps backward.

"What do you want, Alfred White?"

Alfred's heart started palpitating.

Pacific was right. A part of Alfred didn't want anything to do with the shady fellow who knew when people were going to die. It was the same part that wanted to fill out papers in the security of his cubicle. And yet, another part of him wanted the opposite.

So what did *he* want?

Alfred looked at the tombstone in front of him.

"Your face is turning as white as your name," Pacific pointed out to him. "Are you going to be sick again?"

Alfred swallowed hard. "I ... I'm fine," he said, his voice wavering. He looked at Pacific, trying not to blink.

Pacific, a man who seemed to exist outside the fabric of reality, who could rewind time at his own pleasure, who sought death as a commodity. A puzzle wrapped in a mystery.

In a matter of weeks this man had upended Alfred's life. In a way, Pacific had awakened Alfred, showing him where his life was headed: into a descending spiral of regret and sorrow.

But.

There was so much more than that.

What price was he willing to pay to continue his journey with Pacific? What was the trade-off for the knowledge he was seeking? A slow walk on the rim of madness?

He had no idea what Pacific had in store for him. Alfred knew he might not be ready for it. But he didn't care.

He was not going back now.

"I don't want to end up like them," Alfred finally said. "I don't want to be the one tearing pages apart. I want to change. I want to learn. I'm willing to sacrifice what I am now for the promise of who I might become."

Pacific looked at Alfred for a long moment, and he smiled. "Then you might," he said simply. "Come, my promising protégé. There is someone I really want you to meet."

8

HODIE

They walked off church property and back to the residential neighborhood. Pacific glanced up and down the street then hailed a passing cab.

"Saint Expeditus Hospital," Pacific instructed the driver as he and Alfred got in the back seat.

"I'm hungry," Pacific said to no one in particular when the driver started the engine. He began searching inside his coat. "Are you hungry?"

"Not really," Alfred said.

"Where did I put them? Oh, yes ... Here."

Pacific emerged with a bagel, a zipper bag with banana chips, and a small water bottle.

"Where did you get all that stuff from?" Alfred eyed the food suspiciously.

"A coat is worth only as much as the number of pockets it hides," Pacific said while munching on his bagel. "And mine hides many."

Pacific finished the chips and the bagel in less than two minutes then drank eagerly from his water bottle.

Alfred realized only then how thirsty he was. "Can I have a sip of that?" he asked. "Is it water?"

"Water?" Pacific raised an eyebrow, looking at Alfred with amuse-ment. "Do you think I'm some kind of plant? Water is boring."

"Okay." Alfred rolled his eyes in exasperation. "What *exciting* thing are you drinking, then?"

Pacific peeked inside the container. "Here I've got two delicious raw eggs blended with a ripe avocado, blueberry, spinach, banana, and carrot juice, if you want to sip at this ambrosia." He offered the bottle to Alfred, who tentatively sniffed at it.

"Good grief!" The young man jerked his head back as if struck by an invisible punch.

"What?" Pacific looked at him curiously.

"It smells like a used pair of socks filled with fresh vomit." He raised a hand, warding away the awful smell. "I'll pass, thank you."

Pacific shrugged off Alfred's comment and continued drinking.

For the next five minutes, the tune on the radio lulled Alfred's thoughts into a stream of blurred images and sensations.

He looked out the window at the city streaming by, an ever-changing mixture of people, cars, and buildings.

Alfred was thinking quietly but profoundly of events up to that point. He lifted a hand and realized it was shaking, a remnant of the dark feeling that had seized him just moments before. He balled his hand into a fist. "You're not in Kansas anymore," he whispered to himself, amused by his own thought. He looked up and found Pacific looking back at him.

They remained in silence for what seemed like an eternity. Then Pacific put his small bottle back inside his coat, took off his sunglasses, and started polishing them with a piece of cloth.

"You have a question," he said matter-of-factly. "But you are afraid to ask it. There are no safe questions anymore, Alfred White, only dangerous ones. You can either venture and ask it, or let your skull burst open with unsatisfied curiosity." He smiled, as if envisioning the event happening right there and then. "Either way, I'll have fun watching you deal with your thirst for knowledge."

Alfred shifted uncomfortably on his seat and glanced at the driver, who was busy talking with somebody on the phone. "Could you have saved him?" he asked in a low whisper. "I mean Steve. Could you have done anything to avoid his death?"

"Ah." Pacific nodded. "We get to that at last." He kept polishing his sunglasses with a swift movement of his fingers. "Before I answer, you have to understand something important. A piece of information without which everything falls apart."

"What is that?"

"An undeniable fact of life," Pacific said gravely. "All human beings are born with a specific time balance. It can be eighty years or eight minutes. It doesn't matter. When the time balance turns to zero, your life ends."

"A time balance?" Alfred asked, puzzled. "What do you mean by that?"

"Think of it like a bank account balance," Pacific said. "When your bank account has zero money left, you are broke. So it is with time. When your time account balance is empty, you're dead. This is the easiest way I can explain it to you. Some are born with a very limited time balance. Others have plenty of time before death kisses them goodbye."

Pacific ran a hand idly over his smooth chin. "Now on to your question. You're asking me if I could have *saved* Steve." He pronounced the word *saved* carefully, as if it were something balanced on the tip of a very tall mountain. "Yes, I could have," he admitted. "I could have saved him because I know how to handle time, and I have some to spare. Remember what I said? Death is a commodity, a resource that can be used. But ..." Pacific put his sunglasses back on.

"What?" Alfred said eagerly. "But what?"

"When you see a beggar on the street, do you empty your pockets for that person just because he or she is asking you for money?" Pacific looked at Alfred expectantly.

Alfred shrugged. "Of course not," he said. "But I don't really understand the analogy. We're not talking about giving a few dollars to a homeless guy so that he can buy a beer or two. We are talking about saving a life."

"There is no difference to me," Pacific said, a smile brushing the sharp corners of his mouth. "I'm not a charity, my young friend. I'm a business owner. A successful business owner, at that. Obviously, I don't deal with money—I deal with time—but the basics are the same. Like any successful business owner, after many years of activity I've managed to save a surplus I can use as I please. But I don't go out and squander it. Time, like the money in your wallet, is a finite resource. In fact, time is our scarcest resource, and one of the most mistreated assets available to man. But this is the point. Scarcity makes it a precious and hard thing to give up for someone like me, who knows its true value. You see, you don't give money to a beggar, because you know he is going to waste it on booze. But you could lend some hard-earned time to a select group in exchange for something useful to you. Or you can do the opposite: ask for some time in exchange for something the person needs, something you can provide. When it comes to a time transaction, the sky is the limit."

"You said *something useful to you*," Alfred pointed out. "What would that be?"

"A favor, a connection, a word said by the right person at the right time. A door opened without asking too many questions. It could be anything I need at that moment. It's hard to hammer a nail without a hammer, don't you think? The need changes as the situation calls for it."

Alfred's head started spinning. He rubbed it and squeezed his eyes shut. "So you're saying that you can give your own time to others, or you can get time out of people in exchange for something else?"

"Yes." Pacific bobbed his head once. "I can take time away from other people or give away some of my surplus of time, depending on the situation."

"But only if you know you're getting something in return."

"True again."

Alfred thought a bit about that. "So you could have saved Steve by giving him some of your time. But you didn't, because—"

"He had nothing to offer me," Pacific said simply.

"Right." Alfred nodded awkwardly, trying to wrap his head

around the idea. It wasn't easy to think about time that way, but it made a strange kind of sense. It was like one of the many projects Alfred had worked on in the past few weeks. Some of them didn't get past the evaluation phase and never saw the light of the day. Projects without potential were thrown away and left to die in the trash bin.

"What about the day of the déjà vu?" Alfred asked suddenly.

"What about it?"

"You said you use time as a currency, and that time demands time in return. Does it mean that the day of the déjà vu, you used some of your surplus to rewind time?"

"Very good." A smile broke onto Pacific's face. "You're digging deeper. Yes, I had to use time to bend time to my liking. So I did yesterday, to embed the lemon in the reality of its moment. Quite an investment, now that you point it out."

"You did that just to get my attention?"

"I had only one chance to make a strong first impression." Pacific darted a teasing look at Alfred. "Obviously I did. You're here talking to me. Aren't you?"

"So you spent time to convince me to listen. What if I'd decided to simply ignore you and go about my life?"

"The risk was there," Pacific admitted. "Every endeavor has its own risks, my young friend. It's true. I took a risk by offering you knowledge, and I got rewarded by sparking your curiosity."

Alfred glanced out the window and gathered his thoughts before asking another question. "Is there a way to keep your account balance filled past your natural life span?"

"Ah, that is the mother of all questions," Pacific said with delight. "But I won't answer it right away. I challenge you to stretch your mind further. Think bigger than that. Much bigger. What's better than having your account balance filled past your natural life span?"

Alfred didn't immediately get what Pacific was hinting at. Then it dawned on him. "Is there a way to keep your account balance filled indefinitely?" he asked.

"Ah!" Pacific's smile was so wide it nearly split his face in two. "Very good. An easy idea that comes to mind if you follow your own line of thought, isn't it? Yes, Alfred White, you could potentially keep death at bay for as long as it pleases you."

Alfred's mouth had turned dry. There he was, inside a cab, heading toward an unknown destination and talking about immortality with a fellow who had the power to bend time.

The thought should have unsettled him, but after witnessing time shift a few times and seeing a person dying in front of him, the list of things that could unsettle him was shrinking rapidly.

It was a while before Alfred finally mustered the courage to ask the question that was on the top of his list. "How old are you, really?" he asked, not bothering to hide his curiosity.

Pacific leaned forward intently, smiling a mischievous smile. "Now that is a very insolent question, Alfred White."

The cab stopped. Alfred realized it only when the driver turned toward them, waiting to be paid.

"Mr. White," Pacific said. He got out of the cab without a second glance.

"Right," Alfred sighed. "Credit, please."

Once he'd stepped out of the cab, Alfred looked at the vast, imposing building that stood in front of them. It was the color of sand and was surrounded by a huge parking lot with cars moving about. An ambulance was taking off from the ambulance bay at that moment, its sirens turned on. Cars moved away from its path.

"From a graveyard to a hospital," Alfred commented solemnly. "This is not going to get any better, is it?"

"Don't look so grim," Pacific said, nudging Alfred mildly with his elbow. "You have to strike while the iron is hot. Your mind is raging now. Trust me. This is the best moment for you to bathe into knowledge."

"That, or I'm going to have a heart attack," Alfred murmured gloomily.

Pacific moved toward a statue that stood at least ten feet tall near the main entrance of the hospital. Alfred slowed down and studied it.

It depicted a man wearing a long, red cloak. Underneath the cloak there was armor, which looked vaguely familiar to Alfred. The warrior was holding a palm leaf in his left hand, and a clock inscribed with the word *Hodie* in his right hand. His left foot was stepping on a crow, which had the word *Cras* engraved upon it.

"The patron saint of this hospital," Pacific explained, answering Alfred's curious look. "Do you know the story of Saint Expeditus?"

"Never heard of him," Alfred admitted. "Is that Latin?" He pointed to the two words engraved on the statue.

Pacific nodded. "Yes, it is. Expeditus was a Roman centurion who was martyred for converting to Christianity. He is considered to be the patron saint of speedy cases and expeditious solutions, and the enemy of procrastination. The legend that surrounds his story is rather interesting. According to tradition, Expeditus became a Christian and was beheaded during Diocletian's Persecution. The day he decided to become a Christian, the Devil took the form of a crow and told him to postpone his conversion until the next day. Expeditus stamped on the bird and killed it, declaring, 'I'll be a Christian today!' You see, the word *Hodie* means *today* in Latin. *Cras* means *tomorrow*."

"I might be wrong," Alfred said, his expression carefully blank, "but I suspect it's not a *coincidence* I'm staring at a statue with a story so related to my ... What did you call it? Oh yes. My mentorship."

"Every story has a lesson," Pacific said, smiling his assent. He made a quick gesture toward the statue. "What do you think is the lesson to be learned from Expeditus's story?"

Alfred crossed his arms as he looked at the statue. "Refuse Satan, I guess?"

Pacific smiled dryly. "That was a safe bet. Refusing Satan is part of the story, of course, but there is more to it. Like every story worth remembering, Saint Expeditus's story is about choices. But this one is also about timing. There would be no statue in front of us today if Expeditus had listened to the crow and postponed his conversion. Do you see my point?"

"Not really."

"You should. The choice you made back in the graveyard brings you closer to Expeditus's story. You chose to walk the unknown and didn't bend to the voices of refusal and procrastination. You willingly decided to venture into a dark forest you know nothing about for the promise of what lay at the end of it." Pacific put both hands on Alfred's shoulders. "By the end of this mentorship," he continued, looking intently at Alfred, "you will be very glad you started this journey. Your understanding of my world will continue here, as we unveil another important piece of information. At this point, you know that time can be used. For a price."

"Yes," Alfred agreed. "Time demands time in return. If you want to use it, you need to get it first."

"Not only that." Pacific showed Alfred his wristwatch. "You also need a buffer to use it."

Alfred looked at what up to that moment he had thought of as a useless piece of garbage. "So that is the source of your power?" he asked, looking perplexed. "That watch?"

"Not the source," Pacific corrected him. "The supply. This watch holds the time I use. Bear with me. A gun remains a gun without ammunition. You just can't fire anything with it."

"So you are the gun, and that watch is your bullet?"

"Sort of."

"Okay," Alfred said, trying to follow Pacific's explanation. "But how exactly do you harvest time?"

"With much planning." Pacific spoke slowly, picking his words with care. "It's not as simple as raising a flint blade and cutting off the grain. You can't get time out of thin air. There is a process in place that makes things more difficult. There are three rules that can't be broken when it comes to time harvesting. Rule number one: you can only get time out of people. Rule number two: the person you're interested in must willingly give up his or her time to you. Rule number three: once the time has been transferred, it cannot be returned."

"Who or what made these rules?"

"Who or what made the universe?"

Alfred shrugged his ignorance.

"Different people have different ideas on the subject," Pacific said. "I'm not here to debate the color of the air with clever semantics. Remember, I'm a business owner. I just do time transactions and benefit from them. Time harvesting has its own laws, just like gravity, and free will is as unmovable as the opinion of a stubborn god. Do you understand this? I cannot possibly take time from a person without his or her consent."

"But how do you ask people for their time?"

"You don't ask everybody, only a select group," Pacific explained. "It's a tricky subject, this one. Who in their right mind would willingly give up their time? It all comes down to timing, planning, personality, and, well, blind luck, to be completely honest. Most people don't know the real value of time, others underestimate it, and some others are blinded by the need of the moment and give up time easily in exchange for something valuable to them. Time buys you possibilities. People live as if they were not aware of the clock ticking. And most of them end up wishing they had a different life, in the end. Mind you, every person has a different story and is at a different stage of their life. In some stages, a few people regard time as less valuable than other things. That is the best moment for me to approach them and make an offer they can seldom refuse."

Pacific turned his back to Saint Expeditus's statue and walked toward the hospital's entrance.

9

A GEM IN THE DARK

The inside of the hospital was warm and well lit. There were nurses bustling around and doctors busy talking, and a broad variety of people from the outside world just waiting in line or sitting and staring at big screens with numbers on them.

As Pacific and Alfred moved past reception, Alfred also noticed people dressed in long, blue robes, wearing identical pairs of white slippers. They didn't seem to have any destination or task to accomplish. They moved around aimlessly or sat and looked at passersby with dull eyes and faces bathed in boredom.

"Have you ever spent time in a hospital?" Pacific took off his sunglasses, folded them, and put them inside his pocket.

"Once, as a child, I had a post-operation recovery," Alfred said, shrugging. "Nothing more than that. Why are you asking?"

Pacific looked around, his eyes taking everything in. Alfred could sense a strange excitement radiating from him, as if the tall man had just stepped inside Wonderland.

"Hospitals are places unlike any other," Pacific explained, gesturing grandly with both hands. "They are realms of shadows creeping inside a person's mind. Worries, needs, the fear of the unknown. It's everything here! If you spend enough time inside a hospital, you will know what I mean."

Alfred frowned. *Realms of shadows creeping inside a person's mind?* he thought, unimpressed. That was a bit melodramatic, even by Pacific's standards.

"I'm aware hospitals are not exactly fun places," Alfred said, "but I don't think they are *that* bad."

"Bad?" Pacific echoed him, sounding affronted. "You misunderstand me. I love hospitals! I love the jaded atmosphere that makes this place so glorious in its monotony. I love the bland walls and stark lights that tire the eyes and wreck the soul. I love the buzz of gossip and the complaints about treatments and medicines and the lack of empathy. Most of all, I love the chemical smell embedded in every room and every corridor." Pacific half closed his eyes and sniffed the air noisily. "I love the endless possibilities of time harvesting a place like this offers. I've closed some of my best deals inside hospitals."

"Deals?"

Pacific gestured around happily. "Hospitals are a great place for time harvesting if you know where to look and the timing is right," he said. "A good eye for detail is paramount, of course. If you possess it and do your homework, you might find yourself sitting on a pot of riches."

"You're losing me," Alfred said. "Why exactly is a hospital getting you so pumped up?"

"Put it into prospective," Pacific said patiently. "A person could cross that door alive"—he gestured toward the entrance—"and never see the light of day again. It's not difficult to find people begging for a ring buoy in the storms of their life. When a person is sick, their way of seeing the past, present, and future changes dramatically. They want a rope to rescue them from their predicament. The fear of emerging from this place weak, mutilated, or altered terrifies them. And the closer they are to death, the stronger is the fear."

Pacific stopped in front of an elevator and called it. "Always remember," he said while they were waiting. "A person who thinks they have all the time in the world can be inclined to give some of it to me if I'm very shrewd and play my cards right. But it won't be a sizeable amount of time. Those small transactions are almost never worth the effort. What I really seek are desperate people with their back up to the wall, people with no choices left. Hospitals are one of those walls. One needs to look deep and hard, but the most valuable gems are buried in the dark."

The door of the elevator opened, and they went in. Pacific pushed one of the buttons to the upper floors.

"So you don't only consider one person's need," Alfred said. "You also factor in where they are."

"That is correct," Pacific said. "Some places put people in a mindset that I can exploit to bend their will more easily."

"What kind of places, besides hospitals?"

"Asylums are another great example," Pacific said. "So are nursing homes, prisons, and, believe it or not, casinos. The list goes on and on. Anywhere that imposes a time constraint on life is a potential cash cow for me."

Alfred found himself shivering. He was all too aware they were talking nonchalantly about something very unsettling. He knew a guy at the Spear, a shrewd financial adviser who preached about how much effort he put in to ensure his client's financial well-being. He was lying, of course. Everybody knew he was just after their money. Alfred felt as uncomfortable with Pacific in that moment as he had with that man at the Spear.

"I see," Alfred said, not really knowing what to add. He opened his mouth then closed it. He stared ahead, wishing the door of the elevator would open soon.

"You look aghast," Pacific commented. "I'm not sorry I'm exposing you to the truth, but I'd like to know if you are regretting your decision to move forward with the mentorship. You owe me that much."

"No," Alfred replied hastily. "I'm just thinking. It's a lot to take in, you know?"

"Oh, I know," Pacific agreed. "Do you understand now why I needed to test your resolve before proceeding? I'm exposing you to a difficult truth. I'm doing it slowly and deliberately. Yet there is no easy way to digest all the information and not be affected by it. When you swim underwater for too long, your lungs will eventually start burning, seeking oxygen. That is when you need to come up for air. We don't want to start gasping for air, now, do we? The moment you feel that the burden of this knowledge is getting overwhelming, tell me, and we will take a deep breath. Do you understand?"

"I'm fine," Alfred said stubbornly. "I don't need to stop, thank you very much."

Pacific looked at Alfred for a while, then he curled the corner of his mouth slightly. "Very well, then." He started rummaging inside his coat. "Take this." He handed Alfred a pack of tissues and a small bottle filled with a transparent liquid.

Alfred looked at the two objects with a puzzled expression. "What do I need these for?"

"These are remedies for tears and blood," Pacific said carefully. "Keep them handy. We'll need them soon enough."

Alfred simply nodded and put them in his pocket. He wished he had the courage to ask Pacific more but found himself devoid of the urge to know.

The door of the elevator opened. Alfred was the first one out.

The upper floor was decidedly less busy than the main floor. There were only a few patients going around, and just a handful of nurses. There was a waiting area on the left of the elevator, with a bench and a couple of wilting plants. A woman wearing pink pajamas was talking on the phone, and a child was playing with toys beside her.

Alfred followed Pacific, who seemed to know where he was going. They turned left after the first corridor, then right, until they reached the middle of a very long corridor, where they found a nurses' station with women and men busy running that part of the hospital.

Pacific looked at a big wall clock hanging above the nurses' station.

"Nice timing," he said. "She should be here by now."

"Who should be here?"

"The gem in the dark."

One of the nurses noticed them. "Can I help you?" she asked hurriedly, writing on a clipboard.

"We're here to visit Miss Hera Alanis," Pacific said. "And we know where we're going. No need to show us around."

"Please sign here," the nurse said, pointing to a sign-in form. Pacific scribbled something on the paper.

"Come," Pacific said to Alfred.

As they were walking, Pacific looked at the room numbers displayed on each door and stopped in front of the room farthest from the nurses' station.

"Well, then." Pacific put a hand over the door handle as he winked at Alfred. "Let us continue our quest for knowledge." He opened the door and stepped inside.

The room was small and bare. The only light came from the outside. It was muffled by a half-closed curtain.

The first thing Alfred noticed was a young girl with long, dark hair sitting beside a bed. Then he noticed another girl lying unconscious on the bed, the upper part of her head covered by bandages. A narrow tube was attached to her nose. Both of them looked young—and strikingly alike, now that Alfred thought about it. They had the same pale skin, as if the blood had been drained from their bodies, same round ears, same aquiline nose.

Even with the scarce light and the bandages that partially covered one girl's head, it was clear the two were twins.

"Close the door," Pacific ordered.

Alfred did it.

The tall man moved forward, his steps quick and sure. The girl who was sitting didn't turn, or move, or do anything that suggested she was aware of them. Her eyes were open and lost, as dull as a piece of tarnished metal.

"Sophia Megan Alanis," Pacific spoke loudly.

The girl started. She turned sharply and looked at the newcomers as if two ghosts had appeared out of thin air.

"Who are you?" she demanded. She stood up and looked at them with an expression that was a mixture of surprise and annoyance.

Pacific stepped forward. "Father Jude sent me," he simply said.

An icy silence filled the air. Sophia looked at Pacific, her eyes gleaming with an emotion Alfred couldn't describe. Reverence, maybe. Or plain fear?

"It's you," she breathed out, as if that was her first carefree breath in a very long time. She slumped back on the chair, looking stunned. "Yes," she said, her expression now a mix of shock and gratitude. "I was waiting for you." She looked at Alfred, as if she were noticing him for the first time. "Who is he?"

"One of my ancillaries," Pacific said dismissively. "He will assist me."

Sophia nodded, as if that explained everything.

Pacific drew up a chair beside Sophia and looked at the girl on the bed. "How is she?" he asked in a practical tone.

"She's dying," Sophia said, casting a sideways look at Pacific. Only now that he was closer did Alfred realize her eyes were wet and swollen. She must have been crying for a very long time. "The doctors say there is nothing else they can do," Sophia added.

"They are right," Pacific said matter-of-factly. "Nothing they can do."

Sophia stared at Pacific. "But you can help, can't you?" she said, her eyes so full of hope they were sad to watch. "Father Jude told me everything."

Pacific placed his DSLR camera on the bedside table. When he looked at Sophia, his eyes were two drops of steel embedded in a white mask. "I know what you want, Ms. Alanis. But I need to make sure you understand the terms. All of them. Father Jude explained to you the consequences of—"

"I don't care." Sophia cut him off. "We don't have time! And I'm ready. This was not supposed to happen. It's my fault. It's all my fault!"

And then Sophia started crying, a long, deep cry that seemed to make the room darker and smaller. Alfred looked away. He felt like he had intruded on something very private he had no business meddling with.

Suddenly, the room grew quiet, as if somebody had turned off a switch.

Alfred looked back at Sophia with eyes wide open. The girl seemed to have turned into a statue, still and silent, a curled figure with her face deep in her hands. A woman in grief embedded in the reality of the moment.

Time had stopped.

Alfred's eyes met Pacific's, and he saw rage behind them.

"Don't you dare look away from her," Pacific hissed, his words as sharp as steel striking steel. "Aren't you here to understand my craft? How are you supposed to do that if you look the other way when the time comes to see more closely? Look at this!" Pacific pointed at Sophia. "This is something I can mold into the shape I see fit. See the sorrow? See the desperation? See the cry for help? Do you see them?"

"I do," Alfred said, nodding hastily. "I see them."

"Good. Because *this* comes included in the knowledge package you requested so eagerly yesterday. See that?" Pacific pointed at Sophia with a sharp nod. "This is what makes me *me*. Now pull yourself together and answer my question. Why am I here?"

Alfred looked at the unconscious girl on the bed. "To ... to harvest her time?" he said weakly.

"Wrong!" Pacific said sharply. "What are the rules of time harvesting?"

Alfred went over them quickly. Then he understood why Pacific had asked the question. "She can't agree to anything," Alfred realized.

"Precisely," Pacific said. He gestured toward Sophia. "That means I'm here for her."

Alfred nodded slowly. "What are you going to do now?"

"Nothing she doesn't want me to do."

The desperate cry of the girl once again filled the room, and Alfred knew that the flow of time had been restored.

"Tissues," Pacific said curtly, holding a hand out in Alfred's direction.

Alfred looked at Pacific's hand for a few seconds before realizing

Pacific was talking to him. The young man patted his pockets and took out the pack of tissues. Pacific handed one to Sophia.

"She's dying because of me," she said between sobs. "It's on me. I did this to her."

"Father Jude told me what happened," Pacific said in a reassuring voice that felt as smooth as olive oil spread over silk. "It was an accident."

"No!" Sophia's breathing was ragged. "It was my fault! I was the one driving. I started arguing and ... I didn't see the red light and ... and ... when the car hit us, I made it out with barely a scratch, while Hera ... she just ..." Sophia trailed off, leaving a void of grief in place of the unspoken words. She shook her head and remained quiet.

Pacific bobbed his head a couple of times and respected Sophia's silence with studied grace.

It was clear to Alfred that Pacific was acting: nothing more, nothing less. The words he spoke, the pauses he used, the reluctance in his voice—everything was carefully orchestrated to give the illusion of empathy.

"I want to make things right," Sophia said finally, looking at Pacific with fire in her eyes. "I would do anything to save her."

"So I've heard," Pacific said hesitantly, looking away with a grave sigh.

"I want her back," Sophia said with a steadier voice. "Please help me."

Reluctantly, Pacific looked back at her. "Do you understand the terms?"

"Yes, I do. I swear I do. Please help her. *Please*."

"Very well, then." Pacific opened his jacket and took something from one of his many pockets. This time it was a knife. Alfred squinted at it, as if he couldn't quite decide if the object were real or not. It was the most peculiar knife he had ever seen. The blade was as black as coal, and the hilt was ivory white. The short blade was thin, but it didn't look frail. At all. On the contrary, it looked sharp and dangerous, like a hornet's sting thrust into the night.

"It won't hurt," Pacific reassured Sophia, who was eying the knife fearfully.

Pacific took the glove off his right hand, and as soon as the black blade touched his skin, it opened a long cut that let red liquid out. He held the blade in his palm, using a tissue to keep the blood from dripping. "See," he said, smiling reassuringly, "I barely felt it. Now your turn, Miss Alanis."

Sophia stretched out her hand and took the knife.

"That is not a normal blade," Pacific warned her. "It's very sharp. Don't apply too much pressure. It could easily cut your hand off if you press too much. Just brush your skin lightly. That is all you need."

Sophia nodded. She looked at Pacific. He nodded back at her with a reassuring smile.

Sophia breathed in and cut her palm.

"Good," Pacific said, his eyes anchored on hers. "Now let's shake on it."

Sophia lifted her bloody hand and shook Pacific's.

A noise from the wall attracted Alfred's attention. It was a low hum, almost a buzzing. Alfred lifted his head and noticed that the room clock was acting weird. The hands of the clock were moving impossibly fast counterclockwise.

He looked at the malfunctioning clock, then at the handshake happening in front of him. Something kindled in his mind. He took his phone out of his pocket and looked at the time displayed on the screen. It was noon ... and then eleven in the morning ... and then it was ten past nine o'clock.

Alfred looked back at Pacific and Sophia.

"It is done," Pacific commanded.

Alfred looked up at the wall clock. It had resumed its normal pace and displayed the real time. *The real time.* Alfred found himself lingering on that thought. What was real, when something like this was possible?

"The bottle," Pacific said, breaking Alfred's reverie. "Give it to me."

"Right," Alfred said. He handed the small bottle to Pacific, who opened it. He poured some of the content on his wound and some on Sophia's wound. The blood stopped flowing immediately, and the cuts disappeared as if they had never existed.

"The Pact of Blood has been sealed," Pacific announced in a definitive tone, putting the knife and the bottle back inside his coat.

Sophia nodded thoughtfully, as if a new realization had dawned on her. "Thank you," she said, her eyes still shiny with tears. "Thank you so much."

Pacific rose. He looked at Sophia's sister. And then it happened.

Hera woke up. It wasn't a sudden awakening; it was slow and progressive, like a person gently woken by the increasingly intense daylight.

Sophia put both hands over her mouth and stared at her sister as palpable relief flooded her face.

She darted toward Hera, took her hands, and kissed her twin on the forehead.

Alfred realized he had held his breath for several seconds, his eyes fixed on the scene.

"Time to go," Pacific said, gesturing toward the door. He turned and walked away from Sophia.

"Wait!" Sophia said.

Pacific stopped. He looked over his shoulder and waited.

Sophia seemed out of words for a moment. Then, mustering a new courage, she asked, "Are you ... Are you really him? Are you Samael?"

Pacific looked at her for a very long moment. "I am whatever you need me to be, Ms. Alanis. But I'm truly nothing more than the blessing of a second chance." Pacific touched the rim of an imaginary hat and bowed slightly. "Yours, always."

Pacific walked out of the room, with Alfred trailing behind him.

10

CROSS OF ASHES

A lfred glanced repeatedly over his shoulders as they walked away from the room.

"You're looking back like some malignant force is chasing you," Pacific said, adjusting the strap of his camera around his neck. "There's nothing back there, Alfred White. Nothing but a done deal."

"I—" Alfred closed his mouth then opened it again, but nothing came out. He bit his lip and tried not to look like he wanted to bury himself underground.

"I don't blame you for the silence," Pacific said. "I blame you for not being upfront about it. Are you still following me in your quest for knowledge?"

"Yes," Alfred managed to say. "It's just … I don't …" he trailed off, waving a hand, trying to chase some thought that kept evading him. "I'm not used to seeing miracles, that's all."

"Miracles? Is that what you think happened in that room?" Pacific's smile was stretched, almost mocking. "No, my young friend. Miracles have nothing to do with my business. What you saw was simply the way of my trade. Nothing more, nothing less. You witnessed a time transaction between a vessel and a donor."

"A vessel and a donor?" Alfred repeated numbly.

"Myself and the girl who sealed the Pact of Blood." Pacific showed the hand he cut with the knife. "Oh, don't give me that look, now. I'm just using the right words to describe what happened. There is a whole new vocabulary you have to familiarize with if you want to truly understand who I am." They walked past the nurses' station toward the elevators. "It's like learning a new language. If you're not open to the culture that harbors it, you'll never fully understand its many nuances. The economy of time is a vast, complicated subject. You just got a peek at it in that room."

"The economy of time?" Alfred echoed, looking lost.

"It's a system based on the sourcing, supply, and distribution of time," Pacific explained. "In the economy of time, everything is based on time balance. Time can be measured, parceled, transferred, or simply used, as I did when I created your déjà vu."

"So that girl, Sophia. She transferred time to you with ... a bloody handshake?"

"Sealing a Pact of Blood requires much more than a cut and a handshake," Pacific said. "It requires free will by the donor. Without that, the time transfer cannot happen."

Alfred nodded. "Well, she looked very eager to give up her time. That's for sure."

"That is why it worked," Pacific explained. "If the donor is willing to give up their time, you can transfer it smoothly. You just need a bridge that can carry it from point A to point B."

"A bridge?" Alfred said. He looked quizzically at Pacific. "You?"

"Remember what I said? Time can be treated as a currency, and a currency can be transferred, if ..." Pacific trailed off meaningfully, tapping his wristwatch. "If you have a reliable way to store it."

"But how can you do that?" Alfred tried not to sound like he was desperate for an answer. "I mean, I get it. You can store and use time thanks to that watch, but how can you decide how much time to get? How can you move it from here"—he waved around frantically, as if pointing at the whole world—"to there?" He indicated the wristwatch. "I just don't—"

Pacific held up a hand, and Alfred stopped talking. "Let me tell you about time," he said. "People keep track of time in very basic terms. Human terms. There are immensely vast and complicated areas of reality that move on different timelines. Some species of insects are born, mature, give offspring, and become no more in a matter of days. The face of the Earth is changing as we speak, a few inches at a time. This is enough to radically change the face of the planet over the millennia. Humans are people-centric, and they devised a way to create the illusion of time control. In fact, they built a prison they willingly live in. No matter what people think, their idea of time is just an artificial package."

Alfred held his hands out. "So what is time?" he asked.

"Time is a river," Pacific said with certainty. "You can take out that river water with your bare hands and call it a minute, but it'll still be just river water. It slips away from your hands if you don't know how to hold it. And to hold it, you need a bucket."

"A bucket?"

"Yes," Pacific said. "This brings me back to square one, which is the need for a reliable system, one you can bank on. A bucket holds water effectively. The economy of time is a system: a bucket that holds time and turns it into an asset."

Alfred half closed his eyes in consideration. "This is much more down to earth than I thought," he admitted. "It seems like I'm talking with my project coordinator."

"See?" Pacific said. "I'm just a fellow operating in a very niche market."

Pacific called the elevator and they stepped inside.

Alfred's mind lingered on Sophia. "How much time did she give you?" he asked as the elevator brought them down.

"Ten percent of her remaining life span," Pacific answered promptly. "Approximately seven years."

"And is that ... a lot?" Alfred asked.

"It's more than average, less than exceptional," Pacific said. "Now, to get back to the mentorship bit, which is what you should focus on, did you notice the girl's state?"

"Yes," Alfred said. "She was very sad."

"She was desperate and broken," Pacific corrected him. "I've provided her with the solution to her problem. I'm happy. She's happy. Her sister is happy. It's a win-win. So you see, a solution to a pressing problem can do wonders when it comes to time harvesting. As I said, timing is a huge factor that can make or break a time transaction. Keep that in mind, and you'll have figured out most of what I do."

They got off the elevator. Once again, they were on the main floor.

Alfred had so many questions he could not keep them all straight. He pondered a little, and plucked a question from the top of the messy pile. "Who is Samael?"

"It's just a name," Pacific said bitterly, dismissing the matter with a casual wave of his hand. "A name with no more real value than *Devil* or *Satan* or *Lucifer*. People have called me by many names, all of them designed to give them an illusion of rationality. I don't like those names. They are dangerous. They nail you down to a set of basic assumptions, and you can't wrestle free of them without becoming something else or disappearing into nothingness."

"But you do have a name," Alfred pointed out while they were passing the cafeteria. "Don't you?"

"That is different," Pacific said. "I chose that name for myself. It's mine. I own it. Nobody stuck it to my face without my permission. The bottom line is that I ignore all the other names—and you should, too, if you don't want to get lost in a dark forest. Trust me. It's dangerous to think you know when you are only assuming."

Something else popped up in Alfred's mind as he was thinking about the time transfer. "That girl, Sophia," he said. "She seemed to know you already."

"Yes," Pacific confirmed. "She knew everything she needed to know about me, and she was well aware of what I could offer her. She had been prepared for that moment long before I walked into that room. That saved me time and effort. I almost never approach a donor who has not been made aware of what I can do."

"She also seemed to believe blindly everything you said," Alfred pointed out.

"People of faith are my favorite stock," Pacific admitted with a thin smile. "They require the least explanation and the least effort to convince. They simply believe, because that is what gives them assurance. And their assurance fattens my purse."

"But ... why? I mean, she clearly had never seen you before."

"That is correct."

"So who told her about you?"

"Ah." Pacific sighed with satisfaction. "That would be my dutiful pastor of souls, the very person I want you to meet."

Pacific stopped in front of a big oak door with a cross engraved on it.

Alfred looked at the door. It took him a few seconds to realize they were in front of the hospital chapel.

Pacific placed both hands on the door and pushed it.

"No words of warning this time?" Alfred asked, trying to brace himself for whatever was waiting on the other side of the door.

"None are needed," Pacific said, pushing the door all the way in. "Relax. Nothing weird is going to happen."

Alfred couldn't bring himself to believe that.

The chapel was spacious but bare. There were a dozen lines of benches, all of them empty. On the opposite side of the entrance an altar sat on a platform, and above the altar, prominently displayed on the snow-white wall, was a crucifix made of gold.

The only person inside the chapel was a priest, who was sweeping the floor with a broom.

"Forgive me, Father, for I have sinned," Pacific announced loudly as he strode in, shadowed by Alfred.

The clergyman paused, threw Pacific and Alfred a careful look, and resumed sweeping. "A sinner is good for business," he said, his voice quick and sharp. "Especially if he brings with him a promise of redemption."

"He does," Pacific said, chuckling. "He does indeed." He looked up. His eyes lingered on the crucifix. "My oh my. That wasn't there last time."

The priest followed Pacific's gaze. "You're right," he said, collecting a bunch of cigarette butts in his dustpan. "We had it mounted the day before yesterday. It's bigger than the last one. And brighter."

"Makes for a better show," Pacific said approvingly. He looked at Alfred. "It's fitting, making a dying man nailed to a board the symbol of a religion that rewards pain and discomfort above all, don't you think?"

"Is this him?" the priest regarded Alfred with a look so quick it was almost a glance. "The bee in the beehive?"

"Apologies," Pacific said, spreading his arms. "I'm forgetting my manners. Alfred White, this is Father Jude. He helps me run my business."

"Hello," Alfred said. He stretched out his hand. The priest ignored it. His eyes remained fixed on Pacific.

"How much does he know?" he asked, his voice edgy.

"He knows enough," Pacific said.

The priest stopped sweeping. "So you decided to go on with him?" The clergyman's jaw tightened visibly.

"Isn't it obvious?" Pacific shrugged. "He's here in front of you, isn't he?"

Father Jude snorted. "We don't need him. I have already told you."

"Your judgment is clouded by pride, Father. We do need him."

The priest leaned the broom and the dustpan on a nearby bench. He turned to face Pacific. "Why?" he asked with more than a hint of resentment in his voice.

"Time has been lagging for a while," was Pacific's answer. "Instances are scarcer and more difficult to find than they used to be. You know this song—don't make me sing it to you again. We need to expand quickly, and we need to do so by planting a flag in a new soil."

"And you think *corporland* is the solution to your problem?"

"Corporland?" Pacific repeated, amused.

"You know what I mean," Father Jude said bitterly.

"It's difficult to see," Pacific admitted, "but there is potential."

Father Jude nodded, but with a tightness that made the gesture look forced. He started rubbing his brow as if to ward off a headache.

"What if I had a case that could buy you more time that you have been able to harvest in a while?" he said, almost whispering the words.

Pacific looked at Father Jude intently. "In that case, I would listen."

The priest briefly bowed his head then pressed a palm to his heart. "I've been working on this case for quite a while now," he said slowly. "It's a young couple. Early twenties. They have a daughter, a four-year-old kid named Sasha. The doctors found a malignant tumor in the middle of her brain stem. She has less than three months left to live. First she will stop walking, and then she will stop talking. And then she will die in the caring arms of her parents."

Pacific nodded thoughtfully. "What are the hook and the stake?" he asked.

The priest breathed faster, and his face gathered shadows. "That is where the thing becomes tricky." He paused, and seemed to choose his next words very carefully. "They are not part of the herd."

Pacific frowned. "Are you meddling with non-believers?"

"They are good people," Father Jude added hastily, "with kind hearts and—"

"No fear of the Almighty," Pacific cut in, his words as heavy as a lead hammer. "What good are they to you? You have no leverage over people with no faith. You know what happened the last time you ventured into uncharted territory. I shouldn't have to point this out to you."

"This case is different," Father Jude said stubbornly.

"How so?"

"I know I can convince them. I just need time. Listen, I know I can do it. I just ... I just have to work a bit more on this case and not rush them into doing anything too bold. I have to twist the story so that it makes enough sense to them that they can see you and be ready for the taking. You know how it works. I don't want to dump info on them, but at the same time, I can't take anything for granted. That would scare them away when the harvesting comes. If they agree, we might be talking about a sizeable deal."

Pacific didn't seem convinced. "How sizeable?" he asked reluctantly.

"Forty years," Father Jude said. "Maybe more."

"A promising case," Pacific admitted. "I'll grant you that. But it's not enough."

"What you mean?" Father Jude's frustration was plain. "It's more than you have—"

Pacific raised a hand, and the priest swallowed the rest of the sentence. "I know what you're thinking, but it makes no difference. Don't you understand? Even if you do succeed with this case, I need more than an occasional windfall to keep the boat afloat. I need an entirely new, reliable flow of income."

"And you think this corporate drone can provide that?" Father Jude blurted out, pointing at Alfred.

"Excuse me?" Alfred said, looking up and squaring his shoulders. "I have no idea what is going on here, but I'm not—"

"Quiet."

Pacific had spoken the word in little more than a whisper, but there was an edge to it that felt dangerous, so Alfred closed his mouth.

Pacific looked back at Father Jude. "Fair enough," he said. "You are scared. I understand that. But you don't have to be. Nothing is going to change."

"Scared?" Father Jude said, sneering at Alfred. "Of him? Nonsense."

"I'm not trying to replace an asset," Pacific said slowly, as if explaining something to a child. "I'm just acquiring a new one. That's all."

"But I—"

"I will not hear more of this from you, Father," Pacific said in a definitive tone. "You've made your point. I listened and found it lacking. End of the story."

Father Jude's jaw twitched angrily for a moment, and he said with a forced smile, "As the fallen Angel of Death commands." His bow was so low, it was mocking.

Pacific ignored his pretentious gesture. "Now that this matter is settled, shall we begin?" he said. "Or do you have any other words of wisdom?"

"None that will make you reconsider, apparently."

Father Jude went to the entrance door and closed it with a key. Then he went to the window and opened it all the way. He took a cigarette pack from his pocket, tapped the bottom, and pulled out a cigarette. He lit it and took the first pull.

"Did you get it?" The priest half closed his eyes in pleasure.

Pacific nodded. "I did."

"All of it?" Father Jude asked, his voice shaking.

"Everything went as planned."

"Glad to hear it." The priest breathed in a heavy breath, and the tension seemed to flow away from him. He pulled at the cigarette a couple of times more. "I'm ready," he said.

Pacific moved the crown of his wrist watch. The priest's expression was eager, his eyes focused on Pacific's wrist watch as if he were staring at the very last star in the universe.

Alfred looked intently at Father Jude, bracing himself for whatever was about to happen.

But nothing happened. Pacific stopped tinkering with his watch and simply said, "It's done."

Father Jude sighed with relief. "Good." He pulled joyfully at his cigarette. "Very good."

"That should calm your nerves better than your nicotine will." Pacific gave a comforting nod to the priest. "There's nothing better than knowing your piggy bank just got filled, right?"

"Would somebody care to tell me what's going on here?" Alfred asked, not happy being ignored for most of the conversation.

"Of course, of course," Pacific said. "Now that we've taken care of the business bit, we can move on to more—"

A cell phone rang. Alfred glanced at his pocket, half expecting it to be Mr. Solidali. But it wasn't his phone ringing. He looked up at the priest, who was still smoking. It was Father Jude's phone.

The priest looked at his phone with eager eyes. Deep lines

formed on his forehead. He was reading a message. The phone kept ringing.

"Who is it?" Pacific asked.

"No one important," Father Jude said dismissively, turning the ringtone off. He put the phone back in his pocket.

Pacific was not satisfied with his answer. "Take the call," he said. It wasn't a request.

Father Jude held his cigarette unsteadily between his index and middle finger. The tip of the cigarette shook so hard that the ash fell on the ground.

"Do it now."

Father Jude took the cell phone out and placed it against his ear.

"Yes?" he said.

Alfred saw his expression pale. It changed from anger, to fear, and back to anger in the space of a few seconds.

"What?" he ground out. "Goddammit! You should have— Well, it's too late now, isn't it? No! Stay there! He's here with me. We'll be there ASAP."

Father Jude turned off the phone. He did not look at Pacific.

"Speak," Pacific ordered.

"It was Joshua." He spat more than pronounced the name. "He was ... calling from the asylum." Father Jude swallowed. He took a pull from his cigarette and went on. "Apparently he decided to move on with the Geminium case." He paused. "Today."

Pacific's eyes narrowed. "I told him to wait until tomorrow."

"He decided to go for it now. And, well ..." Father Jude put both hands over his hair. "The whole thing blew back on him. Big time. He needs help confusing traces and cleaning up the mess he made. Like, now. People noticed what he did, and how. They might trace it back to us."

"Did you have something to do with this?"

Father Jude made an outraged face. "I would never—"

"Careful now." Pacific's voice was sharp. "You know how I deal with useless lies. Speak the truth."

Father Jude dropped the cigarette butt on the floor and stepped on it angrily. "I ... well. I merely suggested ... a different objective," he said, lighting another cigarette. "One that I thought had more potential." He continued talking under the penetrating eyes of Pacific. "I ... I trained him personally. We had everything planned. I wanted to present you with more time for—"

"Fool," Pacific said harshly. The priest recoiled as if struck by an invisible punch. "He hasn't been trained to bend a will. He doesn't know how to seep fear into a person's heart and knows nothing of twisting words and winning minds. He knows nothing of my craftsmanship. You sent a starving hyena to do the job of a bloodhound."

"I didn't mean to—"

"Silence."

Alfred looked at the both of them. "What is happening here?" he asked.

"Idiocy is happening," Pacific said sharply. He looked at Alfred, then at the priest, who was staring at the floor. "There is a change of plan," Pacific said, dragging out the words. "An unforeseen event has happened, and I need to intervene to put things right. It looks like we'll have to end our day sooner than I expected. You see, it happens that I have—"

"Are you seriously trying to explain things to him?" Father Jude blurted out. "We don't have time! We need to go now!"

Pacific faced Father Jude, his eyes cold and unforgiving. "Rush," he said, slowly and deliberately. "You're trying to rush *me*."

The priest flinched. "I ... I was just saying that—"

"You lied to me," Pacific said, as dangerously as a knife brushing over a bare chest. "You disobeyed my order, and now you're trying to rush me." He pronounced the last part of the sentence as if it were an unspeakable crime. "You've grown insolent and bold, priest. The fault is mine. I've treated you fairly. Too fairly, maybe. It looks to me like you need a reminder of the nature of our relationship."

Father Jude backed away. "No." he held out his hands with a dismayed expression. "Please. I was just trying to—"

"You have forgotten the terms of our agreement." A sliver of annoyance ran through Pacific's sharp tone. "Allow me to refresh your memory."

Father Jude staggered to his feet. "Please," he said as his body convulsed and his face contorted in pain. "I don't—"

The priest cried out in agony as he crumpled to his knees. Alfred backed away, watching the scene unfolding in a mute stupor.

"You are nothing but an engine that keeps my wheel spinning," Pacific's stated coolly. "Show me you understand. Show me!"

"I am an engine that ... that keeps your wheel spinning," Father Jude exhaled, bowing his head in submission.

"Master."

"I am an engine that keeps your wheel spinning, master."

"Tell me. Who keeps the demons of regret at bay when they besiege your dreams and sour your sleep?"

"You, master."

"Who keeps your life running past the call of destiny?"

"You, master."

"Who keeps the fabric of your story whole and preserves the meaning of your name when the shadow of the past would reclaim it?"

"You, master."

"Who keeps death at bay for you, Patrick?"

"You! It is you! Only you, master!"

Pacific walked toward the dustpan, bent over, and took a handful of cigarette ashes. He spread the ashes on Father's Jude forehead, forming a cross. "Remember that you are dust," he said, "and unto dust you shall return if you displease me."

Father Jude cried a low cry.

"Rise," Pacific ordered.

The priest rose on unsteady legs, looking at the floor in shock, his face marked by tears.

Pacific pulled his head up and forced him to look at his face. "We're bound together," he said, as if he were stating a universal truth. "You will be alive as long as you serve me well. I am a fair master, but I will not tolerate any more of this rebellion. Do you understand?"

Father Jude mumbled something inaudible.

"Say it!"

"I understand, master."

Pacific let go of him, and Father Jude bowed low. This time, there was no arrogance in the gesture.

"Wait for me in the car," Pacific commanded. "I will be there when I'm done here."

"As you wish, master."

Pacific turned slowly and unwillingly to look at Alfred. He had a peculiar expression on his face. To Alfred, it looked like hunger. It was like a carcass had been taken from a lion's paws just before the beast could sink his teeth into it.

"That was something you were not supposed to see," Pacific said, dusting the ashes from his hands. "A messy situation, my business can become at times."

"What the hell happened? What was all that about?"

"I have no time to explain. But I want you to remember what you learned today. Freeze it in your mind. Remember the power of the knowledge you have unveiled. Don't ever forget this simple truth: time is power. You now know part of the story behind it."

Pacific curled his right hand into a fist, and suddenly Alfred realized that the feeling of being surrounded by water, which he had experienced the day before, had disappeared. He looked at Pacific, perplexed. It was like something between them had been suddenly interrupted.

Pacific had a sour expression on his face.

"I have no franchise over you now," he said. "So I'm asking this of you as a favor. I will be in front of the main entrance of the Spear tomorrow at noon. If you want to finish your mentorship, meet me there. There is one last thing I want to show you."

11

PROVIDENCE

Alfred walked out of the Saint Expeditus Hospital and looked around.

There was a bus station not too far from the main entrance. Any bus would have brought him into the financial district in less than twenty minutes. He ignored them.

He could have hailed one of the many cabs parked nearby. He ignored them too. He felt like walking, so he walked.

The long walk home was slow and uneventful. On the surface of things. On the inside, Alfred's mind was a magma chamber filled with pressure and ready to fracture. It was quicksilver moving relentlessly inside a shaken bottle. It was, in short, a complete mess of thoughts.

He felt like the day with Pacific had started a year before. Ten years before. Maybe a lifetime before.

His mind was trying to sort things out, to make sense of what had happened.

He now knew what before he had only suspected. Pacific was not merely an odd man with a knack for showmanship. He had an entire world hidden behind his back, and in that world, Alfred was lost.

"A lord of time," Alfred murmured, as if saying the fact would make it more real. He smiled. It still sounded insane.

Alfred was no longer debating the reality of it all. He knew it had happened. The difficult part was to shut down his rational mind and welcome the impossible.

One thing was certain. His life had taken a strange turn. A dark turn.

He knew he had asked for the knowledge, and that Pacific had held his end of the bargain, delivering hard answers. But something inside told him he had no right to live in that new reality.

"You're not crazy," he whispered to himself. Alfred inhaled sharply. He spoke again, this time louder. "You hear me? You. Are not. *Crazy.*"

A woman was passing by at that moment. She glanced at him with concern then started walking faster.

Alfred sighed.

"This is what you get from spending a day with that man," Alfred mumbled to himself. "A one way ticket to the nuthouse."

He felt his phone vibrating. He took it out of his pocket. It was a message from Mr. Solidali. He ignored it, as he had ignored all the previous messages, and instead focused on the time displayed on the screen.

He blinked, surprised that he wasn't really paying attention to the hour but to the new meaning time brought with it.

"A currency," Alfred said. "In ... What did he call it?" He scratched his head thoughtfully for a moment. "The economy of time. What kind of a rabbit hole did you fall into? Geez."

Alfred stopped suddenly, realizing where he was. He looked up at the sign illuminated by a streetlight. Main Street.

The sun had almost disappeared beneath the horizon, and the night was waiting to fall.

As Alfred resumed walking, he noticed other people walking behind him. Men and women strolled slowly, shoulders hunched, eyes far away. Their working day was over, and they were heading home.

Alfred felt strange, looking at them. It was like looking in a mirror but seeing a complete stranger looking back at you.

He was looking at them from a different perspective, now, one less like his old self and more like someone he was only just getting to know.

He felt like he was trapped at a threshold between worlds, too proud to go back to where he came from but too scared to take the last step that would bring him inside a new reality. Pacific's reality.

A raindrop splashed on his neck. Alfred looked up. The sky was stifled by huge clouds amassing around a sickle moon.

What time was it?

When he looked at his phone again, he realized it was dead.

"Great timing," he grunted.

It was getting colder, and Alfred felt tired. He looked around, hoping to hail a cab, but found none. The rain grew stronger.

Alfred put his hood up and walked faster.

While he walked, he passed a person lying on the street, snoring inside a sleeping bag. Alfred stopped, went back a few steps, and looked at the homeless man more closely. Even with the dirt on his face, Alfred could see that he was a young man, probably no older than himself. He was sleeping over a pile of cartons with food garbage all around him. His wrist was tied with a long string to a shopping cart full of garbage.

There was a cardboard sign nearby. It read, "Anything helps. But booze helps best."

Suddenly, Alfred found himself wondering about the man's story. Who was he? Why had he ended up like this? What was the series of events that had brought him there, sleeping on the ground like a stray dog with nothing but the clothes on his back? Then other questions started surfacing. What if Alfred woke him up and started chatting with him? Would he know more about his life? And then, what if he pictured a square while thinking of the homeless guy? Would he see how much time this man had left to live? Would he really have Pacific's power?

This line of thought brought him closer and closer to uncharted territory. If he had the choice, did he really want to know? Alfred thought about it for a second. The answer was yes. Yes, he wanted to know.

But why?

There were several answers. The first one was obvious: he could convince this person to turn himself around in the time he had left. He could change the man's life with that knowledge, letting him know that his time was limited and he needed to use it well.

It started pouring heavily, and Alfred was forced to find shelter. He ran quickly inside the first store he could find. He closed the door behind him, looked around, and found himself inside a liquor store.

"Howdy," an old lady behind a counter said without looking up from the book she was reading. "We close in twenty minutes."

"Okay," Alfred said. "Is there a taxi station around here?" he asked.

"Nope," the old lady replied.

"Any bus that gets to Clayfall?"

"Don't know. Don't use them."

"Do you have Wi-Fi?"

"Look, son, I'm trying to read. If you need anything other than booze, you're in the wrong place."

Alfred ran a hand over his wet air. "Thanks for nothing," he grumbled under his breath.

"What was that?"

"Uh, nothing. I'll take a peek around."

"Suit yourself."

Alfred started wandering around the store, a world made of cans and bottles and wooden boxes with more bottles in them. He decided to wait out the rain, taking his time reading bottle labels and price tags. The biggest section of the store was dedicated to beer. There were countless kinds, with different names and shapes and colors.

He kept walking, past the wine section to the far end of the store, where he found the spirits. It was the smallest in the whole store but the one Alfred was most interested in.

The only thing he remembered enjoying during his university

years was rum. A big, red price tag attached to a couple of bottles attracted his attention. There was a thirty-percent discount on selected brands of rum.

"Do you need any help over there, son?"

"No," Alfred replied quickly to the woman who'd greeted him. "I'm good, thanks. Just looking."

"That's a very good deal," the old lady said, pointing to the bottle Alfred was looking at. "It's a darn good amber filler with spicy notes. Do you like rum, son?"

"Well, I don't dislike it."

"Good." The old lady nodded. "It's on promotion just for today. It's a steal!"

"I'll think about it. Thanks."

"Well, don't think for too long." The lady went back to the cash register. "I'm closing in five minutes."

"Sure thing."

Alfred stared at the bottle, contemplating the amber liquid inside.

Why not? he thought. Considering what he'd been through, he deserved a little something to cheer himself up.

He brought the bottle to the cash register, where the old lady was waiting.

"Good lad," the lady said, smiling a sparsely toothed smile. "No problem this bad boy can't solve. Trust me on this one. I'm gonna need two pieces of ID, though."

"Sure." Alfred passed them over. The lady took a painfully long minute to evaluate them from behind her silver-framed glasses.

"Can't be too sure these days," she said, giving the IDs back to Alfred. "Not an hour ago, I had a couple of kids in here with manufactured driving licenses. They used makeup and high heels to look older. Can you believe that? What kind of rubbish goes on in their head, I wonder. Are you paying with cash or plastic?"

"Cash." Alfred gave her a fifty-dollar bill.

The old lady held the dollar bill up to the light. She touched it to check its texture, then rolled and stretched it a few times. "Broken heart, son?" she asked while evaluating the bill.

"I'm sorry?"

"Your girlfriend left ya or somethin'?"

"What? Girlfriend? No." Alfred frowned. "Why are you asking me that?"

"You kinda look like a guy who was just run over by a bus." She pointed to his clothes. "Your hoodie and jeans are full of dirt. I can smell vomit. And your face is paler than my ass. Only women and buses can do that to a man." The lady chuckled.

"Oh." Alfred awkwardly dusted off some dirt from his clothes. He smiled tiredly and mumbled, "Also time tricksters, I guess."

"What was that?"

"Nothing," Alfred hastily replied. "I just had a very intense day."

"Good," the lady said. "Very good. I wish I'd had more of those when I was younger. They build character. Are you taking your change, or what?"

She had been holding the change for a while.

Alfred took the money and pocketed it.

"You have a nice, chill week," the lady said. She looked outside, to the rain pouring angrily against the windows of the store.

"Thanks," Alfred said. Then he glanced outside and sighed. "Well, at least I won't need a shower when I get home." Seeing no point in waiting for the inevitable, he put on his hood and prepared to face the rain.

"Wait."

Alfred stopped with his hand on the door handle.

"Where do you live, son?"

"Main and Clayfall," Alfred said.

"You're walking home?"

"Looks like."

The lady scratched her cheek absentmindedly. "Clayfall, you said? That's just a few blocks away. You know what? I'll give you a ride home. Didn't get the chance to do my daily good deed yet." She took a piece of cloth and started polishing a liquor display cabinet infested with fingerprints. "Gimme ten minutes."

Alfred still had his hand on the door handle. "That's very kind of you," he said, "but you don't have to—"

"Of course I don't, but I've got nothing better to do. Now wait over there and be quiet for a moment. Won't take long."

"Er ... sure. Thanks a ton."

Ten minutes later, the lady switched off the light in the store, grabbed a set of keys, and limped toward the door. She took a heavy rain jacket from a coat hook and went out.

"Let's go," she said, closing the front door. "My Contessa is right in front of the store."

"Contessa?" Alfred repeated, puzzled.

"That beauty," she said, pointing. It was a Gran Torino as white as a bride's dress.

"Nice car," Alfred commented.

"Sure she is. And she knows it." The old lady winked at Alfred. "Come on. Jump in."

Once they were inside the car, the lady started the engine. They drove away from the store and onto Main Street.

"Name's Freya, by the way," she said.

She stretched out her hand. Alfred found himself staring at the chunky fingers, his body paralyzed by a sudden fear. The image of a bloody hand flashed before his eyes, and he inched away without realizing it.

Freya shot a perplexed look at Alfred. "What?" She looked at her hand. "Do I have shit on my hand or something?"

Alfred blushed. "I'm so sorry." Alfred spoke rapidly, almost stuttering. "Alfred. My name's Alfred." He shook her hand for barely a second and then looked outside, avoiding her inquisitive eyes.

"So," Freya said, driving like she owned the entire street. "Was it a bus or a girl?"

"What?"

Freya gestured toward Alfred's messy look.

"Oh." Alfred couldn't help but smile. "Neither."

"Then what?"

"I don't think you'd believe me if I told you."

"Try me."

He considered simply saying he didn't want to talk about it, but then again, a part of him really wanted to talk to someone. Anyone. Alfred considered Freya for a long moment. She was a bit rough around the edges but a fine old lady nonetheless. She gave him the impression that she was crisp on the outside—just enough to signal to the world that she could not be taken advantage of—but tender and open hearted on the inside.

"Today I saw a person die in front of me," Alfred found himself saying.

"Jesus Christ!" Freya looked at Alfred with wide eyes. "What happened?"

"He just died," Alfred said. "He just screamed and fell to the ground, and then ... and then he died."

Freya shook her head and cursed under her breath. "Well, that explains your face." She then glanced at the bottle of rum Alfred was holding. "And suddenly that booze makes a lot of sense." She smiled a comforting smile. "You okay?"

"Yeah," Alfred said, cracking a smile. "Actually, I feel better now. Unloading the burden a bit, you know? Haven't had the chance to talk about it with anybody. Until now."

"I know what you mean. Sometimes we just need to unwind. Drop the load and just talk, you know? You can talk more, if you want to. I'm a very good listener."

Alfred nodded. "Thanks, Freya." He looked outside, at a world lashed by rain. He was suddenly very grateful the old lady had offered him a ride.

"A waterfall to wash away all sins," Freya commented, tapping at the window with her knuckles.

Alfred turned toward her. "What did you say?"

"Just thinking out loud." She smirked. "Someone I used to know said that when it's raining this bad, it's because the planet is trying to wash away the mischief of gods and men. More the latter then the former, now that I think of it. Men are capable of way worse deeds than any god is. Yeah. That's what he used to say, the bastard."

"Was he a poet?"

"Nope." Freya shook her head. "He was a drug dealer."

"Oh."

"But to be fair, before that he was a teacher. A theologian. I know: from the stars to the stables, right?" She shrugged as she widened her smile. "Life is a fucking roller coaster."

Alfred nodded. "I second that," he said.

The traffic was getting thicker. The cars were slowing down because of the rain.

"You believe in God?" Alfred asked.

"Which one?"

"The Almighty, I guess."

"Oh, *Him.* Yeah, sure." Freya lowered and raised her head with conviction. "You get to my age, and it makes sense to join *that* particular club. It warms my day to know that there are golden gates up in the sky, waiting for me, with a bunch of beautiful angels to look at." She winked at Alfred. "If I'm good enough to deserve it, of course."

Alfred looked away from Freya. "Can I ask you a personal question?"

"Shoot."

"Have you ever seen somebody die?"

"Can't say I have."

Alfred looked back at Freya. "I knew that man was going to die," he confessed.

Freya's eyebrows shot up. "What do you mean, you knew?"

"I knew he was going to die before he actually died."

"What the hell are you talking about, son?"

"I wasn't alone," Alfred said, and was surprised that his voice was steady. "A few weeks ago I met this person. He can do things. Strange things. Dark things. And ... he can see when people are going to die."

The old lady remained quiet for a long while. She glanced at Alfred, as if she expected to find something she could not quite see.

"Weird," she said in the end, pursing her lips. "You don't look high."

"I'm not high," Alfred said, offended.

"You don't look crazy, either," the old lady surmised, studying Alfred carefully.

"I'm not high, and I'm not crazy. And can you watch the road, please? You're making me uncomfortable."

The old lady chuckled. "Don't you worry." She looked back at the road in front of her. "I have a third eye on the back of my head, you know?"

Alfred put both hands over his face. "You know what? Forget it. I shouldn't have said that. No one can understand."

"Look." Freya made a conciliatory gesture. "I didn't want to ruffle your feathers. But you drop a bomb like that and expect me to just nod at you? You should have framed it better. You should have said you had a story for me, one with a capital S. I love that kind of stuff."

"It's not something I made up," Alfred said defensively. "It's real. It happened. I'm telling you, I met a guy who can see the remaining life span of a person. That is why I knew that man was going to die."

"Okay, I hear you."

"You don't believe me."

"I do believe you."

"You're just trying to be kind."

"Look, son. Believing in everything is part of my day job."

"What is that even supposed to mean?"

"Let me explain," Freya said in a placating voice. "When you own a liquor store, you get to know a wide range of people. Some have boring lives, and some have lives that are, frankly, too exciting. They tell me all kind of stories. Weird, fun, awe inspiring, and just plain stupid. Lots of them don't make any sense. Others make me question my whole damn life up to that point." She smiled a warm smile. "Day before yesterday I got this fellow completely covered in tattoos, with pink hair, shallow face, hollow eyes. The kindest person you could hope to have a conversation with. He said to me with a straight face that he had sex with aliens. Venusian, I think they were. Only, up there on Venus it seems they don't call it sex, they call it ... What was it? Interpheromonal congregational interaction or something. That story made my day. Anyway. The point is, I'm not against any kind of story. Stories make people interesting. And you know what? I've never heard of your story, and I'd like to know more."

"I think you're just teasing me."

"The hell I am." She put both hands over her chest. "I'm dead serious. Matter of fact, I can see this thing eating you from the inside. Talking about it will help you. Come on. You have this old fart willing to listen. I wouldn't pass on this chance. Do yourself a favor. Tell me more about it."

"I'll pass, thank you."

"What did you say?" Freya took both hands off the wheel and cupped them around her ear.

"Keep your hands on the wheel, please!"

"I'm sorry," Freya insisted. "I just can't hear what you're saying, son. Try again."

"Okay!" Alfred hollered. "I'll tell you more. But put your hands on the damn wheel!"

The old lady chortled. She put her hands back on the wheel. Alfred started wondering if accepting the ride had been a good idea after all.

"Go on," Freya encouraged him. "Hit me."

Alfred looked at the old lady hesitantly. "Fine," he said. He was trying to come up with a reasonable way to tell his story. "So. This guy who can see when people are going to die, he also has ... a power—"

"Like a superhero power?" Freya interrupted, looking at him expectantly.

"Yeah. Just like that."

"Like, flying in space and blowing up things with your mind?"

"Not quite as scenic."

"Right. So what kind of power is it, then?"

"I was trying to explain it, if you'd let me."

Freya lifted her hands apologetically. "Sorry."

"Yes, well. He can transfer time from one person to another, you know. Like, you can live longer if he takes time from a person and gives it to you."

"So you're talking about a time vampire. Yes?"

"I ... I guess so."

"Okay," Freya said. "Time vampire. Got it. Go on."

"My question is: would you do it? Would you live longer, if you had the chance?"

"What's the point of living longer?" Freya said, gesturing carelessly with a hand. "Immortality is overrated. I'm seventy-one. Seventy-two next week. When you get to my age, you understand that if you want to really enjoy life, you take it one day at a time without asking how many tomorrows you have left. It spoils the fun of living."

Alfred pondered that. "What if you could do other things? Like rewind time, for example," he said. "What if you made a mistake and you could correct it before it became a big deal you'd have to live with for the rest of your life? You could have a second chance. You could craft the life you always wanted. You would never have a meaningless life."

"What's meaningless?" Freya asked. "What's meaningful? Give me a simple definition of both."

Alfred struggled for a moment and failed. "I guess I don't know," he admitted.

"Let me tell you something." Freya pointed behind her back. "There's a homeless guy who has being living a few steps away from my store for the past two years. Name's Marco."

"Yeah, I saw him," Alfred said. "He was sleeping outside."

"Right." Freya shoulder-checked and passed a car in front of them. "You would never imagine it, but he's one of the happiest people I know. He doesn't own a damn thing except a collection of garbage, but he wouldn't change it for anything else. Can I judge the way he lives? Can you? Having more time, or the power to rewind it, doesn't make your life more meaningful. It just proves you can't make do with the time you've been given."

The car stopped so suddenly that Alfred was pushed back by the seatbelt.

Freya stared ahead angrily and hit the horn like it was a punching bag. She stuck her head out the window and yelled at a person who was crossing the street. "Are you color-blind?" she shouted. "Red means stop, asshole! If you want to die, do everyone a favor and get it over with on private property. My tax dollars shouldn't be used to wipe your brain off the street!"

Freya hit the accelerator and closed the window. "What's up?" She looked at Alfred, who was silent. "You lost your tongue?"

"No," Alfred said. "I'm just thinking."

"Think loudly."

Alfred looked at the time displayed on the car. "Do you believe in fate?"

"Fate?" Freya repeated. "Like, before I was even born, we were destined to have this conversation? That kind of fate?"

"Something like that."

Freya shrugged. "Nah," she said. "Too plain and simple, you know? It makes for a boring life, knowing everything had been decided. I prefer to drive with the hands on the wheel instead of sitting in the back, waiting to get wherever I'm supposed to go. Now this time vampire of yours. Are you asking me that question because you think fate wanted you to meet him?"

"I guess so."

The car stopped once more. This time Freya turned off the engine.

"Main and Clayfall," she announced triumphantly. "We made it!"

Alfred looked out the window. That had felt like the longest ride in his life.

Freya noticed Alfred's conflicted expression. "Look, son," she said in a soothing tone. "About your question. I don't know if there's a force out there that controls our lives, or if it's all a fucking mess of choices that pile up on one another. I don't know. What I know is that I'm a member of the free will club, and I believe nothing is inevitable. Ever."

Alfred looked at the web of wrinkles that framed Freya's green eyes, and was comforted by her warm look. "Have you always been a liquor store owner?" he asked her.

"Nope." She shook her head vigorously and smirked. "But that is the most successful thing I've ever been." She leaned back in her seat and gave Alfred a knowing look. "To tell you the truth, sometimes I feel more like a shrink with no paper to show for it. I guess it's something that helps with my job. You know, the listening bit." She laughed at her own joke then grew serious. "Look." Freya considered Alfred carefully. "I don't know you, I don't know what your life looks like, and I certainly have no idea what you are dealing with, but I can definitely tell you need a long night's sleep. And a shower," she added, pinching her nose. She smiled, patted Alfred's shoulder. "Talk with a friend tomorrow, or talk with your family. It'll help."

"I don't have any friends," Alfred found himself saying. "I don't have any family." He looked at the old lady and nodded. "Thanks for the ride. And for the pep talk. Really. It helped a lot."

"I'm glad to hear it, tiger." Freya pointed at the bottle of rum Alfred was holding. "Now go get some of that sweet lava inside your belly. It'll help way more than my babbling, I promise you."

"I will. Thank you." Alfred opened the car door and went outside. Then a thought jumped out at him, and he whirled on the spot and called her out before she could start the car again. "What is your store called?"

"It's called Providence," Freya said proudly. Then she added, with gleaming eyes and a theatrical voice, "Where we sell the finest spirits the city has ever seen and don't judge people for indulging in booze before eleven in the morning. Think of me not as a store owner— think of me as your spirit guide. Thank you very much for your business at Providence."

And with that, Freya closed the car door, waved Alfred goodbye, and drove away in the growing darkness.

12

GUNFIRE

By the time Alfred got home, it was well past nine o'clock. He put the bottle of rum on the kitchen table and realized how hungry he was. He only eaten a Thai crepe the entire day. He opened his refrigerator and found it deserted, so he ordered Chinese food.

While he waited, he took a very long shower. He felt a lot better after.

The food arrived one hour late, cold and wet. Alfred ate it anyway. He was famished. When he was done with the box of noodles, he found a fortune cookie he hadn't noticed before. He broke it, picked up the slip of paper, and read out the content.

"Be careful what you wish for." Alfred snorted. "Aren't we a bit predictable, *destiny*?" He threw away the cookie and went to his bedroom.

He had decided that he needed answers, and the Internet was a good place to start digging. He grabbed a notepad and a pencil and opened his laptop. But he stared at the blank screen for a long while before finally turning on the device.

He fidgeted with his hair, wondering what was the best way to start the research. Then, tired of just thinking, he typed the first thing that came into his head.

He typed the word *Satan* into the search engine. The Internet answered with a multitude of results. Alfred snapped the pencil he was holding. "Shit," he said, staring aghast at the number of results. "This is going to be a long night."

After over an hour of reading, he decided he knew much more about sinister cults and rock music but nothing more about Pacific.

Then he remembered something. He closed all the open tabs and started over.

He typed *Samael* in the search bar.

Far fewer results popped up this time.

Alfred started reading. After less than half an hour, he had learned something interesting.

According to many sources, Samael was an archangel featured in Jewish beliefs and stories, as well as Christian tradition and demonology. He was a guardian angel, an evil spirit, the Grim Reaper, a fallen angel, and a warrior. Samael was said to be the Angel of Death.

Alfred bit at his fingernails thoughtfully. "The Angel of Death," he whispered slowly. Wasn't that what Father Jude had called Pacific?

Alfred spent the next couple of hours searching and learning. Then something else caught his eye. According to one source, "as one of the seven archangels, Samael is imagined as having a special assignment to act as a global zeitgeist, a 'time-spirit.'"

Alfred crossed his arms, deep in thought.

He looked over the notes on his notepad.

The Grim Reaper.

Angel of Death.

Time-spirit.

Alfred stared at the screen blankly, his eyes far away.

Pacific had said he wasn't Samael, just like he wasn't the Devil or Satan. They were just names, he had said. But what if all those names described the exact same thing?

What if Pacific was, in fact, just a fallen angel who preyed on people's lives to get time out of them?

Why had he denied those names so fiercely? Was he lying?

It made sense, Alfred thought. Pacific believed that lying was a virtue; he had said so to Alfred. If he could spread defamatory misinformation that affected a person's livelihood just to get a crepe faster, he could lie for any reason.

Alfred tried to picture Pacific as a supernatural being. It explained a lot.

And yet something didn't add up.

Alfred stretched his arms above his head. He let them fall to his sides with a satisfied sigh. His eyes were itchy. He had been staring at the screen for over four hours. He decided he needed a break.

He went into the kitchen and brewed some black tea. His gaze wandered to the table, where the bottle of rum seemed to be staring back at him.

"I did not forget you," he said.

He looked at his steaming cup of tea then looked at the bottle. He had once heard about a drink called Gunfire, a British cocktail made with black tea and rum. He brought the bottle with him into the bedroom.

At the table, he poured the rum in the steaming cup and sipped the contents. It wasn't as strong as he had thought. He put in some more. Better.

Alfred cracked his knuckles and opened up his laptop again.

"What next?" he asked himself. Alfred drummed his fingers on the table, looking around aimlessly. His eyes caught the wall clock above his bed. "Right." He typed the words *time harvesting*. He got a lot of good juice on the best time to harvest garden vegetables and marijuana buds, but nothing relevant to him.

He tried *buffer of time, economy of time* and *time reaper*. No luck.

He abandoned that line of inquiry. He sipped at his tea and snorted. He poured more rum in it.

"Think." He tapped his temple with his pencil. "Come on. Something more down to earth. Something searchable." He looked back at the screen. "Something people would notice, like ..." Alfred trailed off hopefully, his eyes lingering on the TV across from him sitting on the other side of the table. "Right! The news!"

He typed in *recent weird deaths*.

It was well past three in the morning when he found something that caught his attention. News from a local newspaper. It was about a death at the Saint Expeditus Hospital one year before. The journalist had dubbed it "inexplicable." The patient had been hospitalized for a simple case of appendicitis, and the surgery went well. He had died for no apparent reason. The last person who had seen him alive was the hospital's priest. Father Jude.

Weird thing was, the day after his death, the family found a life insurance policy and a will hidden in a safe. He had never told them of this. But the wife should have known. Why would her husband have hidden that information from her?

That sounded like a time deal to Alfred. Time in exchange for an important favor. Maybe the man was destined to die. Maybe he had been made aware of the fact and decided to give the time he had left to Pacific in exchange for a way to take care of his family after his passing.

Alfred dug deeper. He read websites, forums, and social media. That was only the first of many weird deaths that Alfred discovered in the following hour. Some of them had happened to patients hospitalized at Saint Expeditus. There weren't enough to get the general public suspicious. After all, people died in hospitals every day. But for Alfred, it was different. He knew what Pacific was capable of, and he could see his devilry at work in every piece of information.

The more stories he found, the more he sipped his tea, and the more he sipped, the more he felt like there wasn't enough booze in it. So he added more. And then some more. After a while, as he read, he automatically poured just enough rum to make the tea interesting enough.

Alfred wondered if he was reading too much into those stories. If he was imagining things.

He sipped at his cup and winced. There was only rum left in the cup.

He lifted the bottle of rum and found it very light. "Wow," he said, running an unsteady hand through his hair. "You are a bad boy." He pointed at the bottle of rum as if he were scolding a mischievous kid. "Very bad boy." Then he realized he was swinging on his chair. The world was spinning around him.

"Oh," he said, trying to steady himself. "Okay. Slow. Down," he said. "This was not supposed to happen, damn it." He needed to search for more information. He was so close to getting his answer.

But he felt bone tired. He could barely keep his eyes open.

He took his phone, set the alarm, and put his head on the desk. "Just a couple of hours," he mumbled as he closed his eyes and let oblivion wash over him.

13

A GRAIN OF SAND

There was a familiar man in front of him. He was wearing a blue suit. For a moment, Alfred thought the man was standing as still and rigid as a statue, defying gravity. But he'd gotten everything wrong.

The angle was wrong. His position was wrong. Alfred had been staring with his head cocked to the side, his left ear almost touching his shoulder.

Alfred straightened and looked once more.

The man was sprawled on the ground. His eyes were half-open.

He knew that man well, of course. His name was Steve Rowsons Junior, and Alfred had watched him die.

A crow came from the sky and landed just a few feet away from Steve's corpse. The crow looked at Steve and made a jerky head movement. "Cras," it croaked, spreading his wings wide. "Cras. Cras."

"Go away," Alfred said to the bird. "You hear me? Go away!"

"Cras," the bird answered, twitching his wings. "Cras."

Alfred picked up a rock and threw it at the crow. He missed it.

"Cras!" The black bird screeched louder and louder. "Cras! Cras! Cras! Cras!"

"Shut up!"

The crow shut up. It looked at Alfred, its eye gray with a red rim around the pupil. The eye of a demon.

"You are supposed to stamp on it, you know."

Alfred whirled on the spot. A tall figure clad in black was looking at him.

"What are you waiting for?" Pacific said impatiently. "Don't you know that time is of the essence? Do what you're supposed to do. Fulfill your destiny." And then Pacific smiled a wicked smile, clapped his hands, and disappeared into nothingness.

Alfred jerked awake. He looked around and found the light of a new day creeping through a corner of the window.

The back of his head was throbbing. He touched it with both hands, and a headache bloomed from the base of his neck.

He blinked, rubbed his eyes, and pushed off the keyboard. He looked around, in search of his phone. He found it on the floor, as silent as a dead fish.

It was just one hour before noon. The alarm had never sounded. Instead of pushing the number two once, Alfred had pushed it twice. So much for a quick nap. He had slept well over six hours, and now had less than one hour to get to the Spear. He rose on unsteady legs and walked to the entrance door before realizing he was still in pajamas.

"Right," he said, eyes half-closed. "Clothes first."

Alfred dressed and splashed some water on his face. He looked in the mirror. "I'm ready," he said. "You're ready."

Alfred went out feeling weary and vaguely nauseous.

The city was quieter than usual. The air, too, felt heavier, as if the world itself were waiting for something to happen. Alfred looked for a cab, and found none. He decided to walk down Main Street. He still had some time before noon.

As always, the newspaper street vendor was yelling the latest news. "Woman wakes up from coma!" she shouted while waving a bunch of newspapers to passersby. "Her twin sister commits suicide on the same day!"

Alfred slowed down and came to a full stop. He looked over his shoulder, his heart skipping a beat. For a full minute all he could do was remain on the spot, staring at the lady. He managed to shake himself out of that trance and walk back. "Give me one," he said.

The woman handed him a newspaper, and Alfred took it with unsteady hands. He picked a random bill from his wallet, gave it to the woman, and started walking away.

"Hey, wait!" the woman yelled after him. "This is way too much—"

But Alfred wasn't listening. He kept moving, his mind deep into the reading.

As he kept walking, his breathing became shallow and irregular. He stumbled on his feet several times, and almost fell twice. He read fast, skipping entire sentences, then went back and tried to make sense of what he had missed. After a few minutes of that unfocused reading, he got the gist of the article. Sophia had killed herself the day before. It had happened just after Pacific and Alfred had left the hospital. She had sliced both her wrists and bled to death.

Alfred read the piece several times, hoping every time to read a different story. But the story remained the same.

He folded the newspaper, put it under his arm, and kept walking.

He should have known.

It was obvious, after all.

One life for one life.

If he were the Angel of Death, he could never have passed up on the opportunity.

Alfred was startled to discover that he wasn't as surprised as he should have been. The thought unsettled him. It was almost as if a part of him had known that Sophia was going to die.

Once he was a stone's throw away from the Spear, he paused and looked at the massive skyscraper.

It was strange to be there. Almost wrong. Now that he no longer worked for the company, it was like watching a very tall, very odd collection of glass and steel that looked strangely ominous.

Alfred looked around, searching for Pacific. Eventually his eyes found a man in a dark coat. Like a white shark among salmon, he stood out among the legions of people heading toward the Spear. Pacific was sitting on a low wall made of bricks that flanked the road. He was watching people go through the entrance, his arms folded, his eyes shielded behind his sunglasses.

Alfred walked toward Pacific and sat right beside him.

"I'm glad you came," Pacific said, his eyes still on the main entrance.

Alfred said nothing. He was well aware of the newspaper still under his armpit. It felt heavier that it had any right to be, but somehow it gave him a strange sort of reassurance. It kept him solid and grounded.

"See the entrance?" Pacific asked him.

Alfred nodded. "I see it."

"It reminds me of an hourglass."

Alfred squeezed the newspaper in his hands. "An hourglass." He pursed his lips and shook his head. "Sorry. I don't see any hourglass."

Pacific leaned over and pointed with both hands toward the entrance of the Spear. "Don't you find it amusing, the way people go in? Their *will* to enter without questioning, to follow the stream without caring, to abide by the rule that governs their life with no clue as to the *why*? It's fascinating. And it all starts from *that* entrance."

Alfred shrugged. "Looks like just an entrance to me."

"No, it's not." Pacific moved his hands to form an imaginary square. "It's much more than that. People go into that building like sand flowing through an hourglass. Every single one of them feeds the building with their time to keep it working, to keep the wheel spinning."

Alfred glanced at Pacific. "You sound almost disappointed."

"Disappointed?" Pacific echoed him. "I'm livid. It's such a waste."

"What is it that you want, then?" Alfred asked.

"I want some of that time."

They stared at each other for a while, and then Pacific looked at his gloved hands and said, "You see, Father Jude is operating a dying business. The business of faith." He gave an exasperated sigh. "It doesn't pay as much as it used to. Times have changed. People's attention lingers on other things now: luxury, status, money, fame. Yes, God and faith can no longer be my only viable options."

"Yes. You made that clear enough yesterday," Alfred said. "So what are you going to do?"

"I'm going to adapt," Pacific said with disarming simplicity. "Businessmen need to adapt to the time if they want to survive. I need a new stable source of income, and the corporate world can be that to me. And that brings me to you. You are a bright fellow, Alfred White. You can be my key into that world."

"I quit my job," Alfred pointed out to him.

"No, you didn't." Pacific said. "You missed a couple of days, that's all. I've got a good story you can tell them, and they'll believe you. They will take you back with open arms. I will make sure of that."

"I don't understand." Alfred shook his head. "You're asking me to go back there, to do something you warned me against. Repetition. Dying one day at the time. Remember that stuff? What was the whole point of convincing me to quit if your intention was to get me back in?"

"It wouldn't be the same," Pacific explained. "Think about it. You have gathered knowledge. You know the power of time now. That makes you much more than anything you've ever been before. Before the mentorship, you were a sheep, a part of the flock. What I'm offering you is to become a shepherd. All your life, you have strived to fit in, to be part of the fabric of society. I'm giving you the chance to follow me and be an element outside of the rat race. Don't you see? I can teach you how to get inside a person's mind and turn a mere wish into a pressing desire. I can show you how to drive a confident mind to the precipice of doubt." Pacific looked at the Spear with a reverent expression. "There are countless people inside that building, desperate for a solution to their problems. Many of them will not care about paying in the currency of my choice. I want you to be my agent inside that world made out of wants and needs. You are a creature of that world. You understand the rules. You could listen to the many stories that populate the Spear and take advantage of them in ways that you cannot even imagine."

"Why would I do that?"

"For the same reason you sought me in the first place. To gather more knowledge. To become more."

"More *what*?"

"More than just another predictable story."

Alfred said nothing. He just looked at the Spear and held the newspaper so tight, his knuckles became white.

"Think of what you learned with me in a day," Pacific said. A smile broke onto his face. "Multiply it a thousand fold. I'm offering you the power to influence lives. It's an art I can teach you, something that will set you apart from everybody else."

"I see," Alfred said calmly. "You would teach me those things as you taught Father Jude?"

Pacific looked at Alfred carefully, a smile of amusement playing on his pale face. "You are different."

"I had some time to think over our day," Alfred said.

"And what was the outcome of all that thinking?"

"That maybe I'm not interested in more knowledge after all. I had my fair share yesterday." Alfred handed the newspaper to Pacific. "I read the news," he said. His voice was flat and didn't sound like him. "I know what happened to her."

Pacific took the newspaper. "Oh, yes." He read the title. "Poor thing. A tragic death."

Silence followed that statement. Alfred asked, "Did you kill her?"

"Me?" Pacific stopped reading and looked up at him. "I thought you read the news. The girl committed suicide."

"I know what I read. Answer the question."

Pacific folded the newspaper and placed it beside him. "The girl killed herself by taking a razor to both her wrists and bleeding to death in a bathtub," he said matter-of-factly. "I don't kill people, Alfred White. I trade and grant wishes. That's all."

"You told me she gave you ten percent of her time. Seven years."

"That is the truth," Pacific said. "That was my premium for the time transaction. The rest went to her sister."

Alfred's dry smile soon became a grimace. "I should have expected something like that from someone who lies just to get his lunch faster. There's nothing you wouldn't do for just a little bit of time, is there? By the way, how did it go at the asylum?"

Pacific seemed taken aback by the question. "Things were solved," he said sourly. "And stupidity was dealt with."

"Really? You don't look very happy."

"I'm not. I had to fix a problem and lost much time in the effort."

"I'm sorry to hear that."

"No, you're not. You look fascinated."

"Maybe," Alfred said. "You want to know something?"

"I guess I do."

"It's good to know that even the Angel of Death is not omnipotent."

Pacific looked at Alfred with amusement. "Is that what you think I am?" he asked.

Alfred shrugged. "It's funny how putting a name on something makes it less frightening."

"Ah." Pacific seemed genuinely disappointed. "I warned you about the danger of names, didn't I?"

"What is the danger?"

"The danger is thinking you know something until you find out you're dead wrong."

"Fair enough," Alfred said. "But let's play a game. Let's pretend for a moment you really are the Angel of Death."

Pacific sighed. "Let us," he said in the end.

"Why would the Angel of Death want to harvest time from people?"

Pacific shrugged. "I wouldn't know. I'm not him."

"Indulge me."

"As you wish." Pacific made a vague gesture. "Why would the Angel of Death want to harvest time from people, you ask me. Well, maybe he is out of time, and constantly needs to fill the void that keeps his reality precarious. Maybe his own survival depends on keeping his own hourglass constantly filled with sand."

"A void?" Alfred repeated, puzzled. "Like a wormhole?"

Pacific shook his head. "There are so many things you don't know, Alfred White. It's pointless to try to explain what cannot be explained with words. Your language and your culture are huge barriers you can't overcome by simply asking questions and expecting satisfying answers from me. I'm a good teacher, but I'm not *that* good."

"Always clear in your vagueness," Alfred said bitterly. "Can you at least tell me what happens if the void isn't filled with time?"

Pacific took his sunglasses off. He looked Alfred straight in the eyes. "I cease to exist," he said. "Is the answer clear enough?"

Alfred stared at him. "The Angel of Death ... dies?"

"I told you. I'm not what you think."

"No," Alfred smirked. "You're just a fellow trying to make ends meet, aren't you?"

"That I am."

"You really expect me to believe you, after all I've been through yesterday?"

"I don't have the audacity to expect anything, ever." Pacific put his sunglasses back on.

Alfred paused, considering carefully his next question. "What happens if you die?" he said in the end.

Pacific snorted. "Now you're asking me a question much too pretentious, even if we are pretending."

"How many ancillaries do you have? People like Father Jude."

"Does it matter?"

"It matters to me."

"Not enough," Pacific admitted. He suddenly seemed tired and frustrated. "I need more."

"And that is why we are here," Alfred said.

The wind blew relentlessly. People moved around. Alfred wasn't aware of them. He wasn't aware of anything other than the man that called himself Pacific.

Silence stretched between them for such a long time it seemed to become a material wall, impossible to climb.

"I'm going to say no to your job proposition," Alfred said after what seemed like a lifetime. "I think I'm underqualified for it."

Alfred stood.

"Listen," Pacific said. His voice had lost some of its brio. "You can walk away from me. It's your choice. It's your life."

"But," Alfred said.

"But." Pacific stood up as well. "Bear with me once more, and I promise you the time will be worth your while."

Alfred turned. "Give me one reason why I should care."

Pacific smiled his odd smile. "Let me show you why."

14

THE STORY OF TIME

When Alfred was fifteen, his mother told him God didn't exist. She had looked him straight in the eyes and stated that God wasn't any more real than Santa Claus or the Tooth Fairy. He was just a lie, she had said. Nothing more.

That was long after their dream of making it as musicians had crumbled under the harsh weight of reality, after they had been forced to work three jobs to pay their debts and put food on the table.

Faith had been squeezed out of their life, and sorrow had crushed their spirit.

Yes. His mother had made clear that God had no place in their lives, but Alfred had always wondered if her statement could be proven without a doubt.

Did God exist?

Alfred had never considered himself a believer and had never bothered digging further into the matter. It just didn't hold enough importance for him.

Until now.

Now, Alfred was certain he was closer than ever to answering that question.

Alfred looked around slowly at the beautiful and vast structure that surrounded him.

The inside of the church was welcoming. A stifled light came from glass mosaic windows that depicted scenes of sin and salvation.

Alfred knew that just a stone's throw away from that church, there was the biggest graveyard in the city, the place where his mentorship had begun.

Alfred focused his attention in front of him, where rows of empty benches led to an altar. In front of the altar there was an open coffin, and inside the coffin there was a man dressed in a white suit.

Alfred looked at Steve's face, so still and so pale. The man seemed at peace, and he reminded Alfred of a crafted porcelain doll.

The church was completely empty now. The last person had left shortly after the ceremony ended.

A few people had attended. Alfred had counted fewer than twenty. He and Pacific spoke to none of them, keeping far away at the very back of the church.

When the last few people had paid homage, both Alfred and Pacific had emerged from the darkness, coming forward to face the man they had watched die.

Pacific leaned forward, his gray eyes fixed on Steve. He took the beanie off his head out of respect and put it inside one of his many pockets. Alfred found himself glancing at the man's head. There was nothing but ruffled black hair.

"What?" Pacific asked him with a quizzical look. "Did you expect to find a pair of horns? I've got nothing to hide."

Alfred shrugged. "If you say so."

Pacific studied Steve. "Doesn't it feel like closing a circle, looking at him one last time?"

"You said you wanted to show me something."

"It's right in front of your eyes."

Alfred looked at Steve.

"What do you see?" Pacific asked him expectantly.

"I see a corpse." Alfred looked away. "Are we done?"

"That's it? "

"What do you want me to see?"

"Just what's in plain sight."

Alfred shrugged. "Sorry," he said, sounding anything but. "I just see a dead man in a nice suit." Then he turned to Pacific. "What do *you* see?" he asked.

"I see the last word of the last chapter of the last book of a life. I've always believed that time is just a story made up of a collection of heartbeats. It goes by fast."

"Very poetic," Alfred said. "I will ask you this question just because it's clear you want me to ask it: Why are we here?"

Pacific smiled broadly. "Ah, yes. About that. Our late Steve harbored a story that might be interesting to you. You see, he worked at the Spear, just like you, and he also liked to walk through Aion Park to get to work faster. I spoke with him a couple of times before I met you. He was bolder than you, more stubborn. He never saw sense in my proposition."

"You knew him?" Alfred asked, surprised.

"I knew his name," Pacific said. "I knew his story. But I didn't really have the chance to know him. He was a person I thought might be interested in my mentorship. I was wrong."

"He said no to you?"

"He never got to that stage." Pacific drew in a deep breath and let it out slowly. "He never heeded my call. You are the first one who has stuck to me till this point."

Alfred said nothing. Cold sweat started gathering on his back. So that was the truth, he thought. He was not the first person to fall into Pacific's net.

"Do you now understand why we met?" Pacific asked him, a soft edge in his words.

Alfred looked at Steve. He froze on the spot as realization washed over him. Right there, in that coffin, was his answer.

"Do you understand?" Pacific repeated.

Alfred did. A part of him had always suspected it but never wanted to admit it.

The young man nodded numbly. "Yes," he said calmly. "I'm dying.

Aren't I?"

Pacific nodded. "I've been feeding you with time for a while now."

Pacific was speaking the truth. Alfred knew that. His mind put pieces together so naturally it was almost shocking to realize how they had been in plain sight for all that time. He remembered his cell phone acting up the second time he met Pacific in the park. Pacific had transferred time to him. The same thing had happened at the hospital, when Sophia transferred her time to Pacific.

"I can understand what's going on in your mind," Pacific said, his voice as delicate as a soothing caress. "It's a lot to take in. You would not have needed this last bit of knowledge if it weren't for yesterday's little mess. You were ready to welcome my gift. I could feel it. I'm just making sure you have all the information you need before you decide whether or not to stick with me. The past night might have numbed your resolve, and I want you to focus on the things that matter."

"Why am I dying?" Alfred demanded.

"Does it matter?" Pacific said. "Just know that it's going to happen. Soon."

"Is that why Father Jude is working for you?" Alfred asked. "You're keeping him alive?"

"The priest always had the vice of tobacco," Pacific explained. "He breathes more smoke than clean air. His vice comes with a hefty price. A lung cancer."

"How long does he have left to live?"

"Father Jude is a dead man walking," Pacific said simply. "He was supposed to die years ago, but he has managed to avoid meeting his boss due to his talent for finding good candidates for time deals. He was reluctant at the beginning, just like you. Eventually he saw sense in my proposition. You are a smart fellow, Alfred White. Sealing a Pact of Blood with me is the only way to avoid the coffin. You know I'm right."

Alfred nodded, his eyes blank. He knew Pacific had already won.

"How long will the Pact last?" Alfred asked.

"As long as there is blood in your veins."

"And if I don't do it, you'll just find someone else, right? Like you found me after Steve?"

"There will be no need for further research," Pacific said reassuringly. "You know why? Because you don't want to end up like Steve. You don't want to be just another unfulfilled story. You told me so, remember? You don't want to end up like them." Pacific pointed, with a hand out the window, to the graveyard just outside of the church. "You don't want to be tearing pages apart. You want to change, you want to learn, and you are willing to sacrifice what you are now for the promise of who you might become. You now know the truth, and you know that it's only by defying death that you will finally have true knowledge. Bond with me, and be saved."

"You are right," Alfred said weakly. "I don't want to die."

Pacific's smile was wide. "Say the words, then."

Alfred hesitated an awfully long moment before finally saying, "I think I want to fill that time account balance after all."

Pacific searched inside his coat and emerged with his knife. He took off his glove, sliced his palm with a quick gesture, and handed the knife to Alfred, who took it.

Alfred considered the knife in his hand. It was cold, and heavy. Much heavier than it had any right to be.

Alfred breathed raggedly. He pressed his palm against the edge of the knife and felt an unpleasant tugging sensation followed by a sharp pain. The pain disappeared almost immediately. He stared at his wound, at the blood pouring generously from it. It was a deeper cut that he had meant to make. His hand had been shaky and unsteady. It didn't matter. It was done.

"I am ready," he said. He extended his bloody hand, and Pacific stepped forward to take it.

The hand holding the knife jerked suddenly to the side, and Alfred struck Pacific's forearm. The reaper's hand fell to the ground with a sinister thump, glove, wristwatch, and all.

Pacific's eyes widened with surprise. The scream he made was more inhuman than the sound of a thousand angry wasps forced out of their hive. Alfred didn't waste time thinking. He buried the knife into Pacific's chest. The black blade went easily into his body. Pacific stumbled back, and the tall man wasn't tall anymore. He was on his knees.

Blood poured from the wound. Pacific looked at Alfred, stunned, and stared at the knife buried inside his chest as if he could not believe it was there.

"I will not be another piece on your chessboard." Alfred stepped hard on the wristwatch and broke it under his feet. "Now you can't go back," he said. "Now you can't feed on people's desperation. The circle of death will close."

Pacific mumbled something inaudible and fell to the ground like a sack of wheat. He was dying. Alfred could see it clearly.

Their eyes met.

The reaper made a grimace of pain. Except it wasn't a grimace. It was an odd smile, framed in blood.

Alfred blinked.

He suddenly felt disoriented. He looked around, confused. He was not where he was supposed to be. It didn't take long before he realized …

Alfred was looking at Steve's face, so still and so pale. The man seemed at peace, and he reminded Alfred of a crafted porcelain doll.

"Marvelous thing, déjà vu. Don't you agree?"

Alfred recoiled. Pacific was right beside him, looking at him with fascination.

"That was truly a beautiful death," he went on, one hand over his chest where the knife had been buried just a few seconds before. His hand was back where it belonged, no trace of blood. "I never thought you had the audacity to do such a thing. I am surprised. I'll admit it. Bravo." He clapped his hands theatrically.

"How could you—"

Pacific took off the glove from his left hand. He was wearing a second wristwatch. That one wasn't working either. "When it comes to very important things," he said, "I always keep a spare copy."

Alfred slumped on the floor. "I see." He smiled, amused, and then he chuckled. "Funny." His palm still had the deep cut. Blood poured generously out of it.

"The cut will keep bleeding until there is nothing but empty silence inside you," Pacific said. He took the small flask of transparent liquid he had used to seal Sophia's wound and showed it to Alfred. "Once the cut is there, nothing but this water can heal it."

Alfred nodded numbly. "How much time do I have left?" he asked.

"Ten minutes. Less, if you move." Pacific stepped closer. Once again he took off his glove and cut his palm. "That was an act of bravado. I understand it. You wanted to prove something to me, and you succeeded. You have character, young man. Something I value. However, acts of boldness like that will not save you. Only I can."

Alfred looked at the reaper's hand. It was close. It was tempting. It made sense.

He looked at his own hand. Blood poured abundantly from the deep cut. A pool of red liquid was already gathering at his feet. It made him sick.

Alfred looked back at Pacific. The reaper's eyes were eager.

"You really don't understand, do you?" Alfred said faintly. He moved away from Pacific and felt the world spinning as he walked. "It's not about life or death anymore."

Alfred stumbled on his feet, stopped, and sat on the floor. His breathing became harder. Surprisingly, he felt calm, in control.

"What?" Pacific's forehead furrowed in confusion.

"Life and death don't matter anymore," Alfred murmured. He glanced at his cut.

"You're delirious," Pacific said. His eager expression became perplexed. "What's more important than life and death?"

Alfred looked up. The church had an even bigger crucifix than the chapel's. It was beautiful. He looked back at the reaper. "Salvation," he said, smiling.

Pacific took a step toward him. "You don't understand. This has nothing to do with—"

Alfred shook his head. "No," he said firmly. "I do understand." He pointed at Pacific's hand, ready for the handshake. "And my answer is this." He raised a middle finger.

Pacific's jaw twitched. "What is this stubbornness of yours? You're making no sense at all. Take my hand." Again Pacific extended his bloody hand.

"No sense." Alfred gave a hard, humorless laugh. "What is sense, anyway? Spending a day with you makes that word pretty senseless, you know." He felt his body go numb and his strength abandoning him like water bursting out of a broken dam.

"Don't be a fool, now." Pacific showed a hint of apprehension. "You've made your point."

Alfred looked at Pacific. He squinted, rubbed his eyes. All he could see was a fuzzy figure against a bright mosaic window. "I've learned people are capable of doing drastic things if you drive them to the edge." Alfred took a deep breath, swallowed, and took another breath. "Like planting a knife inside a chest, for example." Alfred looked away and chuckled.

"It's not going to be what you think." Pacific's voice had an edge that made it quiver. "You are not—"

"What?" Alfred croaked. He felt his mouth dry. "You mean, I'm not going to be your slave for eternity?"

"You're not going to be anybody's slave, Alfred White, you are going to live. There are benefits attached to this offer."

"And if I should happen to disagree with you, maybe I will find myself begging you to stop while you torture me?"

"That is simply not—"

"I'm sorry," Alfred said, feeling weaker by the second. "I'll pass."

Pacific moved sharply to Alfred's side. His expression was urgent now. "You're not seriously considering dying on me, are you?"

"I'm sorry," Alfred said again as he felt the life seeping away from his body. He found himself smiling. "I'm just not part of your club."

"Look at me, Alfred." Pacific took Alfred's head tenderly in his hands. "You've gone too far to allow fear to stop you now. Your place is by my side. Shake my hand, and help me keep death at bay for you."

"It's funny," Alfred said. He looked at Pacific with amusement. "I just realized I've never asked you: why Pacific?" For some reason that seemed important.

The reaper looked into Alfred's eyes. Alfred didn't blink or flinch. He let him look inside him for a thousand years and then some.

Pacific released Alfred. He closed his eyes and shook his head. He sat beside his protégé. "I've truly lost you, haven't I?"

"I'm afraid so." Alfred placed a hand on the reaper's shoulder. "Your name," he insisted. "I want to know why you chose Pacific."

"Curious until the very last." Pacific's smile was barely there, but it was the most genuine Alfred had seen on his face.

"Consider it my last wish."

"Fair enough," Pacific said. He dropped the bottle's contents on his wound and covered his hand with the glove. "My story starts with water." His voice was slow and clear, a storyteller's voice. "I was born in the Pacific Ocean on a stormy day that made the Pacific anything but." He looked up, his grey eyes shiny. "No one has the right to wear its name more than I do. It fits me like a glove."

Alfred studied the reaper's face. He could barely distinguish his features now. He wanted to ask him questions, but as soon as he tried to concentrate on the words, he forgot them. He let the other speak.

"The Pacific is larger than the land mass of all the continents combined," the reaper said. "It could swallow them all with room to spare. I am like the ocean. I can retain my identity and purpose, no matter how many names ..."

Pacific kept talking, but Alfred's attention drifted. His words became streams of sound that made no sense at all.

"Alfred?" Pacific's voice was distant, the echo of a thought.

Alfred blinked. "I need a long vacation," he said to no one in particular. "I am so tired. So tired."

Alfred's eyelids felt heavy. He closed them and felt so much better.

Music started playing in the background. "It's beautiful," he whispered. It reverberated inside the church. Or was it in his mind? The music was familiar. He had heard it before. Yes. It was one of his parent's songs, the one he liked the most.

The voice that was calling him went silent.

Everything went black suddenly, and Alfred White finally knew the answer to his question.

EPILOGUE

Names are powerful things few people know how to handle. When you name something, or someone, that thing or that person becomes the name itself. And then it can't be anything but the meaning it's bound to.

A name harbors the promise of a story, and every story has a beginning and an end.

But this story is different. This story has many beginnings and many endings.

That happens when you have, inside the fabric of the tale, a man with many names.

Such a man can cheat destiny and forge for himself the ending he likes best.

A man with many names is a danger to reality itself.

He is a promise of dark things to come.

~

THE MORNING BROUGHT a stark wind that wormed between the buildings of the city like a never-ending snake. The cloudy sky spoke of rain to come, and the streets still wet spoke of rain that was already embedded in the past.

Pacific was sitting on a bench at the center of Aion Park. His eyes wandered aimlessly, not looking at anything in particular and yet taking everything in.

He was a dignified figure, brooding over his latest failure.

"Names," he muttered, disconcerted. He balled his gloved hands into fists. It was because of them that he had failed.

He knew too well that the very nature of a name is a promise, and Alfred White had believed in the promise of a name that didn't belong to Pacific.

The man clad in black straightened up a little. He opened his mouth, closed it. He hesitated for a few seconds. "Samael," he said at last. He paused, letting the word sink in. The name felt wrong in his mouth. It tasted like acid. It didn't belong to him.

Pacific's jaw was clenched tightly. He closed his eyes and breathed in slowly. Then, like he was forcing himself to drink a bitter medicine, he said, "Satan." That felt even worse than before.

For a long while, Pacific went through the painful process of speaking all the names people had used to describe him. All of them left a sour aftertaste.

He abandoned his futile effort. There was no sense to keep trying. He knew all too well the power of a name, but he would never understand the how behind it.

It was like being able to wield a powerful magic sword but having no idea where it came from, or who made it.

It was like a promise. You either believed it or you didn't.

The world was a collection of promises. Pacific knew that. People believed in ideas, gave them names, and suddenly they became stories.

Such is the power of names.

Names can turn an angel into a demon in a blink of an eye. Names can save a life and can start a war. Names are precious, and fragile, and treacherous.

However, all things considered, Pacific knew his failure was a stepping-stone to his final goal. He had lost time, yes, but he had also learned many things in the process.

A boy no older than eight came running toward him.

Pacific frowned. "You're late," he said.

"Sorry," the boy said, trying to catch his breath. "Got slowed down by my granny."

"And where is she now?"

"Taking a nap by the lagoon, as usual. She won't bother us. I promise."

"Good," Pacific said. "Are you ready?"

The boy grabbed a big, red ball from the ground and showed it to Pacific with enthusiasm. "Ready!" he shouted.

"Remember to throw it at my signal, and not one second before," Pacific instructed him. "And for mercy's sake, easy with the swing this time, okay? You almost killed the last one."

The boy laughed at that. "That was fun," he boasted joyfully. "Wasn't it?"

"Yeah, it was." Pacific smiled and ruffled the boy's hair. "Right, you rascal," he said. "Go take your position."

The boy raised a hand to his head. "Yes, sir!" He darted away and hid behind a nearby bush.

Pacific sighed. He looked up to the sky heavy with clouds. He knew it was going to rain. That was not a forecast.

He saw something out of the corner of his eye: a passerby in a hurry. Pacific followed him with hungry eyes, tasting the promise of a new beginning.

"Excuse me, young man," he called, smiling an odd smile that looked a lot like a grin. "Do you know what time it is?

THE END

FOR TODAY'S INDIE AUTHOR, every bit of exposure helps. If you liked *Lord of Time*, then perhaps you could **spare a few minutes to write a review at your favorite online bookseller.** I really appreciate your time. :D Thank you for your support!

SUBSCRIBE TO MY NEWSLETTER

Sign up to my newsletter to get exclusive deals and updates on upcoming books.

http://www.micheleamitrani.com/about

ACKNOWLEDGMENTS

This book owes much to a bunch of people that took some of their time and generously gave it away to make the story better.

I was lucky enough to have critique partners who pointed out things in the story I'd never even noticed, and who went out of their way to give me valuable feedback.

Two of them in particular, Mark and Sev, read the whole story and were kind enough to point out what worked for them and what didn't. They are both talented writers who made my story better in many ways, and I'm lucky I had the chance to know them through the Vancouver Genre Writers group.

A big thanks to my brother and my friends Alessandro, Antonio and Jackson. They read a very early draft of *Lord of Time*, which at the time had a different name and purpose, and made me want to write more about Pacific and the economy of time.

My friend Robin is probably the single biggest reason why I wrote this book in English and not in my native language. He challenged me to write in a language that was unfamiliar and odd to me. The challenge was real, and it was daunting, but after two years of trials and failure, I can honestly say his advice paid off.

Thanks to Benjamin Roque, who designed a cover I just can't stop looking at, and thanks to my lovely Mana, who makes me a better person just by standing at my side and believing in my stories.

Lord of Time was fun to write. I hope you had fun reading it.

Michele Amitrani

Vancouver, July 21, 2019

ABOUT THE AUTHOR

Born in Rome in 1987, Michele Amitrani is a transplanted Roman writer now living in Vancouver, British Columbia. He has grown up writing of falling empires, space battles, mortal betrayals, monumental decisions and everything in between.

He now spends his days daydreaming on park benches, traveling through time and space and, more often than not, writing about impossible but necessary worlds.

When he's not busy chasing dragons or mastering the Force, you can find him at MicheleAmitrani.com or hanging out on Facebook at /MicheleAmitraniAuthor.

Made in the USA
San Bernardino, CA
22 November 2019

60216499R00100